W0043152

EBURY PRESS
YOU ARE ALL I NEED

Ravinder Singh is the bestselling author of *I Too Had a Love Story, Can Love Happen Twice?, Like It Happened Yesterday, Your Dreams Are Mine Now, This Love That Feels Right . . .* and *Will You Still Love Me?*. He has edited two other anthologies, *Love Stories That Touched My Heart* and *Tell Me a Story*. After having spent most of his life in Burla, a small town in western Odisha, Ravinder is currently based in Gurgaon. He has an MBA degree from the renowned Indian School of Business. His eight-year-long IT career started with Infosys and came to a happy ending at Microsoft, where he worked as a senior programme manager. One fine day, he had an epiphany that writing books was more interesting than writing project plans. He called it a day at work and took to full-time writing. He has also started a publishing venture called Black Ink (www.BlackInkBooks.in) for debut authors. He is a fitness freak and loves to play tennis and badminton.

When he is not writing stories, he is creating funny videos for his YouTube channel, SOCHAALAY. The best way to contact Ravinder is through his Instagram handle, www.instagram.com/ThisIsRavinder/

you are all i need

EDITED BY

RAVINDER SINGH

EBURY
PRESS

An imprint of Penguin Random House

EBURY PRESS

USA | Canada | UK | Ireland | Australia
New Zealand | India | South Africa | China | Singapore

Ebury Press is part of the Penguin Random House group of companies
whose addresses can be found at global.penguinrandomhouse.com

Published by Penguin Random House India Pvt. Ltd.
4th Floor, Capital Tower 1, MG Road,
Gurugram 122 002, Haryana, India

Penguin
Random House
India

First published in Ebury Press by Penguin Random House India 2020

Editor's Note © Ravinder Singh 2020
Copyright for individual stories vests with the authors
Anthology © Penguin Random House India 2020

ISBN 9780143429388

Typeset in Bembo Std by Manipal Technologies Limited, Manipal
Printed at Replika Press Pvt. Ltd, India

www.penguin.co.in

MIX
Paper | Supporting
responsible forestry
FSC™ C016779

Contents

Editor's Note

The world is full of stories. We are full of stories.

We tell them every day, many times without even realizing. That's what we do when we write a caption underneath a picture we post on Instagram, or we text a friend about a break-up. We tell stories when we talk to our loved ones, we tell stories when we gather together and think about life gone by, we tell stories when recounting happiness, when we talk of sadness, moments of anger, moments of joy . . .

And then, at some point, we want the other person to tell us their story and we listen to what they have to say. That's when we say: *Aur batao* (tell me more)*!*

You see now? The world loves stories. And I love love stories!

That's what I have been doing for more than a decade now—writing love stories. My readers love them.

They are never done, and there is always space for more to be added. That keeps me going. But I also like to hear from my readers, get everyone together to read a good love story, to connect everyone so they can read together.

Therefore, when I, together with my publisher Penguin Random House India, embarked on this new journey for a collection of short stories, I wanted to hear from you, my dear readers, about your fantastic love stories—and I wanted to bring some of those to this platform, this anthology, *You Are All I Need*.

We took the excitement to the next level when we partnered with Romedy Now, a television channel that I love to watch when I crave romantic movies. We rolled out this campaign, #GetPublished, giving those who love to read love stories, who love to watch romantic movies, an opportunity to get to tell us their tales. And when we did that, what came our way was an ocean of romance. The numbers were overwhelming. After rigorous rounds of elimination, we chose the final twenty-six. These are the best of the best.

And not only are they the best, they are as varied as they can be. If one talks about unrequited love, another tells the story of same-sex lovers; if one talks about love from a distance, the other talks about a quiet love that only reveals itself in actions; if one is about loving and yet letting go, the other is about finding ways to creating the 'happily ever after' with each other.

Together, the anthology is like a rainbow, where each story brings out the beauty of love.

Dear reader, this anthology will leave you with a variety of emotions. And even before you begin reading, I want to place a bet with you. In some of the stories you read, you are going to find yourself; in some you will question yourself; and in some you will simply enjoy the beauty of love. But you will not remain untouched. And when that happens, please find me on any of my social media pages and let me know. I will eagerly wait to hear from you.

Now flip the page and let the magic begin.

With love,
Ravinder Singh

1

A Brief Reunion

Dayal Punjabi

He was astonished at even being recognized. He was so tongue-tied that he stood there like a fool, his eyes as wide and round as a cherry pie. As a schoolboy, he'd never really mustered up the courage to walk up to David, always scared of either being punched in the face or laughed at. They did have a moment, though, when they had been asked to share a presentation on environmental studies in high school. Although David had contributed nothing, he'd showed up on the final day, looked at the slides and blabbered details on the screen as if he knew everything.

Rustom only wished he had a moment where they could share some work again—at least he would be able to handle the uncomfortable silence between them.

'Long t-t-time no s-s-see,' he stammered, wishing he had worn a better shirt or his new shoes or at least a jacket to cover the wet patches under his arms.

'Doesn't really seem like it,' David replied casually with a simple smile. 'Seems like just yesterday we were presenting the three R's of EVS!'

He began unbuttoning and folding the sleeves of his shirt, his eyebrows furrowed because of the scorching sun on his face. A bead of sweat made its way down his forehead, barely missing his left eye. He sucked in his lips.

Rustom couldn't believe how this man, who hadn't even bothered to touch the pen drive so many years back, remembered a moment so brief. A moment he had hoped had vanished by now. He looked at David and then looked away, remembering that there were a lot of people around who knew both of them; perhaps even the unchanged walls of the school building had their memory imprinted on them. The old principal was giving her speech on the tiny concrete stage, her voice fragile.

'So,' David resumed, 'what are you up to now?'

'O-oh,' Rustom stammered again, embarrassed, to say the least. *What would David think if he told him he still wrote stories for a living?* 'Um . . . I'm an author, fiction . . . I write fiction,' he said, managing to find his voice.

'Wow! Sounds fun. Do tell me the name of your book. I'll be interested in reading it,' he said with a sort of pout, obviously uninterested, and then turned to look in front.

There was a round of applause when the speech was over and Rustom joined in. He looked at the carefully combed hair, jet-black and shimmering, and the slim-fit shirt pressing against David's back. His scent was almost hypnotizing, indicative of a masculinity only David was capable of. A slight breeze ruffled his hair ever so slightly and they seemed to dance. He then suddenly looked back, and Rustom went red, like a rose petal.

'What about getting out of here? We could have some ice cream. It's pretty humid up here.'

For a moment Rustom was paralysed, his eyes wide and his lips parted slightly. He couldn't believe those words had slipped out of David's mouth. They'd never even greeted each other when they were in school! He wouldn't know how to talk, to walk or to look better. And even though he'd mentally pictured them walking together, and even though he'd done it plenty of times as a young boy, it seemed so disconnected from his reality now—a lie. He couldn't react at first—it was as if his lips had lost their ability to move and his mind was clouded. His vocal cords felt as though they had collapsed and there was a lump stuck in his throat. He nevertheless nodded.

Before he knew it, they were outside the school building and walking down the sidewalk of the main road, the sound of the city buzzing in their ears, the sun so bright that one could watch the vapour rising in the thick, polluted air. They were walking so close that their hands brushed against each other. David didn't seem bothered at all. But Rustom was flushed; he almost took a couple of steps back. After all, he'd only ever touched him with his eyes. David's skin felt smooth, and Rustom could feel the soft hair on his wrist brush against his skin as their hands touched. From the corner of his eye, he risked a peek at the emotionally distant man walking beside him, and the shadow of a tree fell on them. As they kept walking, the shade stayed with them, and suddenly, almost like an epiphany, Rustom realized he still loved David.

Though it seemed like a lifetime ago that he had yearned for this man, and it had seemed lost when they parted ways, now, with David so close that he could reach out and touch him, Rustom felt like there was no other feeling deeper than this, and that he had never known anything more expansive. Certainly, he thought, no other love had started so far back in time—and now it had only grown and spread throughout his body.

While walking among the sea of people, Rustom bumped into a woman. He quickly mouthed a sorry but the woman didn't bother; she seemed to be in a hurry to get somewhere. But when Rustom turned around to look at David, he was nowhere to be seen. He looked around frantically, a pit in his stomach, as if he had suddenly been abandoned. He panicked and felt unsteady for a moment, and took the support of the tree he was standing under.

This can't be it! I just saw him after years! Is this all it was going to be? I hadn't even spoken to him properly! His eyes began to well up. But then, suddenly, in the midst of the incessant honking of cars and buses, and the un-rhythmic chorus of people, he heard his name being called out. He recognized that voice, even though he'd just heard it, like a brand-new favourite song. He spun on his heels to find the man of his dreams standing across the street, waving at him.

David called out his name again, and Rustom, in dumbfounded fascination, watched his own name form on the lips of the man he'd always wanted. He heard it so close to his ear his body shivered. Everything around them went silent for that moment, and he heard his name again closely, clearly, echoing throughout his being, under his coffee-colour shirt, under his darker skin, so warm and real that his body suddenly went hot.

He raised his hand and waved back. He crossed the road clumsily, almost getting hit by an autorickshaw. Now he was sweating.

When they leaned against an ice-cream truck, David took his vanilla cone, while Rustom took a tiny cup of double chocolate. Then they went and sat on a bench outside a garden. This was what showed Rustom the absolute difference between the two of them, which summed up his hesitation in going up and talking to David in the first place when they were kids. They were opposites! Vanilla and chocolate. North Pole and South Pole. Longitude and latitude. Dark and bright.

And, like always, even now, in this moment when they were sharing a seat, Rustom's voice rang out inside him, praying for some ray of hope. But what sat between them like a ghost was uncertainty. In this clear light of day and the stifling heat and the hoarse cry of the city, silence loomed like a fishing eagle. Escaping that still quietness that had settled on the bench with them would take a reckless roar from inside of Rustom, a vehement articulation of everything he was feeling sitting there beside David.

The silence soon broke like shards of glass.

'What have you been doing all these years, you know, besides writing?' David asked as he sucked on a corner of his melting ice-cream scoop.

The question caught Rustom off-guard. His discomfort grew, with sweat slipping down his face like raindrops from a roof. It uncovered the hollow question of Rustom's own doubts. *What had he been doing all his life that he could even talk about? Especially compared to David's achievements that the entire school knew about.* Rustom always found himself gathering information on David's career as an indie publisher, who published books in the local languages and had blogs written about him. How could he not? It was the only way to know him. And while he kept abreast of David's activities, David clearly had no knowledge of Rustom's dull and obviously less-documented life.

He tried to build up a story in his mind—one that would make his life look livelier than it was. But there lingered a lack of inspiration. He opened his mouth to speak, but then just took a spoonful of his ice cream. And by every drop of flavour that melted on his tongue, he wished they could talk about something else—anything that didn't have to do with his own life.

Thoughts flitted in and out of his ambivalent mind like a fly. Even being a writer did not help Rustom think of something to say that would make David sit up and take notice of him, find him interesting enough. *Just say something! Anything!*

At that moment, David's phone rang and he excused himself, walking away towards the shade of a lone mango tree. He spoke quietly, smiling easily; Rustom could never help himself from falling for it. These were the small things that lingered—the stillness of their new friendship, the air full of thoughts and unexpressed emotions.

Rustom couldn't resist the charm of the man he had once cried for behind closed doors of tiny bathrooms all his growing-up years. David's face stood in his memory, young and beautiful, sure of itself. Such that, even today, it caught Rustom off-guard and held him still, tight, until he reminded himself to breathe again. David's cheekbones were so well defined that even under the shadow of a tree, they cast a shadow of their own on his neck. Rustom watched him, and had the slightest spark of hope, like the flash of a lightning bolt inside his fist-sized heart. It felt as if his eyes were accustomed to just marvelling at the beauty of the imperfect perfection that stood just metres from him.

He had never looked at anyone or anything else, only at him, with an expression that would easily tell anybody around what was in his heart. It was so intense—delicate and adoring but inhumanly strong and divine at the same time.

Perhaps insane.

Soon David was done with the call. He shoved the phone back into his pocket and made his way towards Rustom. He had almost polished off his ice cream and now sat on the bench beside Rustom, munching on his cone.

'Sorry,' he said as it made a crunching sound. '*The wife.* You know how they can be sometimes . . .' And followed that up with a chuckle.

His words pierced the air, and then Rustom's heart so terrifyingly that his body started shivering. Words that had lain like unsaid letters suddenly became bits of torn paper drifting in the wind. He felt like someone had knocked the air out of his lungs. His world all of a sudden had been shaken, and his lips began to quiver.

Of course he is married! What did I think, that he would stay single all these years for me? Me? Someone he barely even remembers?

'She's expecting now,' he continued, 'so she keeps calling to make sure I'm good.'

Shoving the rest of the waffle down his throat, he dusted his palms and then sighed contentedly. 'It's exciting. Scary, to be precise, to even imagine someone like me being a father. Can you believe it?'

But all that David was saying seemed like an echo from a faraway land, for Rustom had ceased to listen. His heart groaned and rumbled like an impending storm. Once again, Rustom hunted for words, for voice, for *something*. But all he could feel was his churning gut. Everything he believed he knew dissolved like sugar in a cup of afternoon tea. He merely smiled. It wasn't as if David wanted to be endorsed by Rustom.

'Hey, I have to leave now, but would love to catch up some other time.' He smiled and stood up. 'Do you have a card or something?'

But Rustom just sat there looking dumbly at the man he had loved all his life and then found out that he was no longer available. But he avoided the urge to just wail and run, and instead dug into his shirt pocket to fish out a visiting card of his authorship that his agent had forced him to get. He handed it to David, who only said 'thanks' and 'see you soon', and walked away.

Rustom watched as David stopped an autorickshaw in the middle of the running traffic, pulled out his mobile from his pocket, with which Rustom's card slipped out and fell on the uneven road, and disappeared from view as the vehicle rounded the corner.

2

Love in Dhavali

Sucharita Date

Love was scarce in the village of Dhavali, mainly because there was no one to love. The lack of money, the unfashionableness of farming and the frustration of village life had inspired a Steinbeckan migration west—from this small unknown village in the Sahyadris to Mumbai.

In search of gold; in search of jobs; in search of people to marry.

But the mad rush to Mumbai hadn't carried Poonam with it, who chose to stay put in the village. She was of the opinion, about the sprawling, daemonic megacity, that it was a place where humans had forgotten their humanity, and she'd promised herself never to set foot in it after her first visit. She preferred being at home with her almost-deaf grandfather, for *anything* was better than Mumbai in her imagination. The young woman spent her days reading, mainly Marathi and Hindi books and newspapers, and occasionally helping a child in his mathematics lessons to figure out how to calculate the L.C.M., or the lowest common denominator.

At fourteen, Poonam had defied her parents' wishes (and commands) and left home to live in a girls' dormitory in Satara so she could complete her education. At that time, it was her grandfather whom she had begged (or, rather, emotionally blackmailed) to pay for her schooling. Her grandfather would still tell everyone how Poonam had grown an alarming shade of purple when she held her breath for 'a whole half-hour' (as per him) when he said no, again and again.

For his investment, however, Poonam's grandfather had expected some returns.

'When will you get married?' he had shouted to her. The deafer he got, the more he shouted.

'When all the men here die,' replied Poonam plainly. 'And then I'll marry a *biptya* or an *asval.*'

You weren't a true Dhavalian if you hadn't had your dog carried away by a biptya, a black panther, or if an asval, a bear, hadn't paid a visit to your farm at night.

Poonam had resolved never to get married. It was difficult to get along as a single woman in those parts. There was no work in Dhavali—and where there was no work, there was even lesser work for women. But that didn't matter to Poonam. She preferred poverty and Dhavali to Mumbai and its riches. Besides, although she had no claim to the little land the family owned, she had her mother's jewellery.

She knew that by avoiding the occasion to wear it, she was avoiding the occasion to sell it.

One day, in the middle of the monsoons, when the rain had halted for a few hours, Poonam decided to sit outside her house reading a book.

'Poonam!' she heard her name being called.

She looked up to see a young man approaching her, and thought she recognized him.

'Vishal!' she exclaimed. 'How come you're here? Are you here to visit?'

As he walked up very close to her, jumping over puddles to avoid the slush, Poonam didn't fail to notice that he took a moment to respond.

'Yes,' he said, when he was in front of her. 'Yes, I'm here to visit.' He smiled.

'For how long?'

'Oh, I don't know.'

'You mean you're here for as long as you please? I can't imagine some rich businessman in Mumbai could be so kind. Listen,' she said, closing her book, 'all rich families run charities, but no rich family is as charitable to anyone as it is to itself.'

Vishal, lost in thought, did not laugh. He said after a pause, 'Well, I'm here long enough.'

Poonam frowned. Vishal was two years older than her, and she had known him all her life. He had been her brother's friend, and had walked with him and Poonam to school. At seventeen, Vishal and Poonam's brother had disappeared to Mumbai to make their fortunes. But while Poonam's brother, when she had last seen him a year ago, had changed drastically and grown aloof and irritable ('It's the pollution,' Poonam's grandfather would say),

Vishal didn't seem to have changed at all. He still had a nervous air about him, as if he was afraid he was being judged.

'Come in,' said Poonam, getting up, but then stopped mid-step. 'Ajoba is inside, asleep.'

'We can sit right here. I don't mind,' said Vishal, sitting on the step next to her.

Two boys ran past them. They had been down to the waterfall. One of them had a string with a crab tied to its loose end. It suddenly struck Poonam that she couldn't recall the last time she'd been down to the waterfall.

'Were you fired?' Poonam asked Vishal in a low voice.

'What?' said Vishal, a little taken aback. 'No.'

There was an awkward silence.

'I quit the job,' Vishal continued. 'Not because I was bad at it—'

'I'm sure not,' Poonam interposed.

' . . . But because I hated it. Poonam,' he said, turning to look at her, 'the first day I reached Mumbai with your brother, I hated it. I hated the crowd, the noise, the people. They don't even speak Marathi there. Can you imagine that? They're in Maharashtra, and they don't speak Marathi.'

'Big deal. You know Hindi, right? Why, all you and Dada did was watch Akshay Kumar!'

'I kept trying to like it, I kept trying to work all these years. But I couldn't take it any more. The city just wasn't for me. I saw that eventually and returned.'

He noticed that Poonam was unaffected by his story. She had taken a long stick and was drawing something in the mud. She didn't rush to offer him her sympathy or support.

'What do you plan to do here?' she asked.

'I don't know. I own land. I could farm fruits and vegetables, maybe.'

'There's a lot to farming, it's not easy. Starting from knowing what your soil's like, and what you can plant there and when, to irrigation, how to sell your fruits and vegetables and where. The people who ran to Mumbai,' she said, gesturing at somewhere in the distance, 'they knew this. They preferred Mumbai to all this.'

Vishal laughed nervously.

'You're smart. But I hadn't thought of all that,' he said.

The compliment brought no smile or blush. Poonam kept drawing in the mud.

'I'll take my leave now,' said Vishal, getting up. 'I suppose I won't get to work immediately tomorrow. You and I can talk often enough.'

'Okay,' said Poonam, without looking up. Something in the way she said it gave Vishal the feeling that she meant the opposite.

For the next few days, Vishal kept his distance from Poonam. It was a week later that he came to visit, and even then it was ostensibly to meet Poonam's grandfather, not her, with news of what Poonam's brother was doing. The only interaction Vishal had with Poonam was the exchange of a nod. This made Poonam angry, but she was quick to realize that the distance between her and Vishal was her own doing, and decided that she should try to be more friendly with him. As she saw him to the door, she addressed a few sentences to him, and even smiled.

Vishal didn't fail to take the message, and over the next few weeks he visited frequently, perhaps a little too frequently for Poonam's liking. It was a strange business—when Vishal was absent, she waited eagerly for him to visit, and when he was present, she wanted him gone within the first five minutes. But she kept this contradiction to herself, and tried not to think about it.

Over time, Poonam and Vishal grew close to each other, though Poonam never cared to admit it to herself.

One evening, after one of their now-routine dinners together, Poonam and Vishal set out for a stroll to walk off the post-meal heaviness.

'Poonam,' said Vishal, 'I've been thinking . . .'

'About farming?' asked Poonam. 'Because the other day I asked Tatyaba, and he said he has some spare seeds. You know, the hybrid ones they make in labs. He said he's not planting them—he's too old to do any planting anyway—and he doesn't mind giving them to you for nothing.'

'No, no,' said Vishal, amused. 'I was thinking about *us*.'

Poonam felt something drop in the pit of her stomach. She had an awful feeling she knew where this was going.

'I think . . . you know . . .' started Vishal. 'I was thinking . . . it might be good to get married. You and I, I mean. No, and before you say anything, hear me out. You are unmarried, I am unmarried. We can work together, and make something for us here. Because you and I have nothing here. Very soon you'll be alone, and—'

'Vishal, I am happy the way I am,' Poonam cut in. After staring at him a moment, she continued, 'And I don't have *nothing* here—I have *everything*. Or at least I have enough for myself. I am happy and secure as I am. I don't need to marry because I am scared of being poor if I don't.'

'That's not what I meant.'

'That's exactly what you meant. That's exactly what everyone means when they advise me to get married,' Poonam turned to him and said hotly. 'I'm going home.'

And she turned around and started to march back home in the dark.

Poonam felt insulted by the proposal. She knew in her mind that she was far too good for Vishal. Here she was, the best-educated person in the village, the most well read. And *he*! Why, he had gone to Mumbai only to return with his tail between his legs, and with no money! Poonam knew that were she to 'help' him run his farm, she would soon find herself responsible for the entire thing. She was far more competent and intelligent than him.

In the following days, Poonam didn't see Vishal at all. Neither had she the time to think of him, for her grandfather's health declined rapidly, and she was occupied with nursing him. But the old man's time had come, and when the doctor was finally called in from Satara, he came home only to declare him deceased.

Poonam's grandfather was cremated. When the pandit performing the rituals told Poonam that only men could be present at the ceremony, she snapped that she had seen her grandfather die, and only she deserved to watch him burn. She had her way.

In the days that followed, Poonam sank into depression. People offered her condolences and tried to make her feel better, but to no avail. It suddenly became apparent to her that she was really, truly alone. Those who said they were there for her knew nothing of the heavy, hurtful *something* that sat on her chest and made it difficult for her to breathe at times. If ever she tried to speak to someone about this sadness, it felt as though she were speaking a different language, for she could never get them to understand her pain. Poonam became increasingly short-tempered, and with every fit of anger sank deeper into sadness.

Sadness and anger—always a great combination for rash decisions. One day, as Poonam was sulking, too agitated to read, she got up from her chair and walked to Vishal's place before she knew what she was doing.

She saw Vishal transplanting rice saplings into the ground, sweating from the labour. When Poonam called out to him, he looked up and smiled. He stepped across the rice bed, careful not to step on the saplings, and walked over to her.

'I meant to come and see you, but I've been busy,' he said, gesturing at the saplings. 'I'm sorry for your loss.'

'Don't be,' said Poonam. 'Even my brother wasn't sorry. Said his employers didn't give him a day off for his grandfather's cremation.'

Vishal looked confused.

'You are working your land?' asked Poonam, ignoring the look on his face.

'Couldn't sit idle forever,' said Vishal, rubbing his hands. After a pause, he said, looking at Poonam with a sidelong glance, '*You* thought I could.'

'I didn't—' Poonam stopped short. 'I just thought that you, maybe, underestimated how hard it was going to be!'

'Well,' said Vishal, 'you definitely can't *overestimate* how hard it's going to be, because it's harder than you can ever imagine.'

'Vishal . . .'

'Poonam . . .'

'I've been thinking . . .'

Vishal's smile disappeared.

' . . . Maybe we should get married.'

Vishal wiped his hands on his pants absent-mindedly, staring into the distance. He then let his gaze settle on Poonam, and did not take his eyes off her for a long time, even though it made Poonam a little uncomfortable.

'Poonam, you don't know what you are saying,' he declared at length.

For a second, Poonam thought she detected a hint of anger in his voice. But only for a second, for she soon realized that it wasn't anger but gentleness. For the first time, Poonam had seen that beneath the characteristic nervousness, there was something far more profound in this man standing in front of her. It was a certain gentleness sprung from strong, unwavering love and respect.

'I do,' said Poonam softly, at a loss for what to say.

'No,' he said with a sigh. 'You are saying this because you are sad and lonely.'

'No, Vishal, I—'

'Do you love me?'

Poonam was caught off guard.

'Do *you* love me?' she asked him, a little incredulously.

'I think you know the answer to that,' he replied with a smile. 'Poonam, I'm not good at putting things into words,

I'll be the first to admit that. But be assured that my proposal came from love and not from wanting a business partner.'

'And now you are rejecting *my* proposal?' asked Poonam, irritated.

'Did I say that?' asked Vishal calmly.

Neither of them said anything for a few moments.

'Do you love me, then?' Vishal repeated.

'Does anyone love anyone when they're getting married?' cried Poonam.

'You don't, then,' he muttered. He looked at his dirty hands, and then at the sky.

'Well then,' Poonam said haughtily, 'I shall take that as a rejection. Goodbye.'

She turned around to leave.

'No, Poonam, wait.'

'What?' cried Poonam. 'Look at you. You say you want to marry me, and then you say you don't. I don't—'

'Look,' he cut in, 'I've been thinking about some things since I started farming. And I realized I was happy you rejected me. Not because I don't love you, but because when your life is changing, it's the worst time to change it more. As in, it's the worst time to get married. So how about we wait? I'll work the land and make something of myself so I can support us. And you can find something to do—you're the smartest girl I know. But if not, you can wait till your life settles down, till you're not so sad. Till then we can wait and see if we, well, can stand each other enough to get married. What do you say?'

Poonam stared at Vishal for a moment, and gave him a slight nod and a smile. Then, without saying anything, she turned and left. Already, she felt the sadness settle back on her chest. But she knew that Vishal couldn't feel it for her. When she returned home, she sat on a chair and opened a book. And thus she resolved to wait out the sadness till her life settled down.

3

The Doors of the Closet Are Now Open

Sai Nithin

The room was more or less the same since our last visit. A painting of a half-naked man hung on the wall. The same certificates, neatly framed, hung beside the painting. The same red–blue–green wind chimes tinkled near the window. The same hourglass stood on the desk; the same old chair creaked behind it; and the same counsellor sat on that creaking chair, helping us solve our problems. It had been fifty minutes now. But what caught my eye was the new picture of a quote that hung on the wall behind the counsellor's head:

That it all began in the days when the love laws were made.
The laws that lay down who should be loved.

And how.

And how much.

—Arundhati Roy

'So, you guys said . . .' Dr Anitha Subramanyam, our marriage counsellor, began, but when she saw me staring at the quote behind her, she changed the topic. 'Have you read the book?' she asked me, adjusting her glasses.

DK, my husband, didn't bother to look at me, or her. So it was on me to carry on the conversation.

'Er . . .' I began. 'Sorry, Anitha, but which book are you talking about?'

Anitha stood up, turned to the framed quote and said, '*The God of Small Things*, of course.'

'No,' I answered.

She looked disappointed.

'Nevertheless, aren't these lines beautiful? You should read the book sometime,' she said.

I nodded, knowing that I would probably never do it.

Anitha picked up her notebook from the table, opened it and said, 'Well, you said that you both met for the first time in school, right?'

DK and I nodded, paying attention for the first time. We had been visiting Anitha Subramanyam for a few days now, without any obvious results.

Anitha placed her notebook on the table. She lifted the hourglass and shrugged, 'Well, your session is done.'

These counsellors are very particular about their session timings, aren't they?

'However, let me tell you this,' she continued. 'Needless to say, there are problems in every relationship, but the solutions to those problems are surprisingly simple. You just have to, you know, look back at the happy times you spent—and I am sure you must have had happy memories too—which now are locked up in your closet. Just open the closet and reminisce.'

Reminisce? Who even uses that word?

DK and I thanked Anitha and started for the door, when she gave us her message of the day, like she usually did at the end of her sessions.

'Sometimes, for love to rekindle, you need to add a pinch of innocence to it.' She sighed and touched the tip of her thumb to her index finger. 'Just a pinch.'

For some strange reason, she sounded like Professor Trelawney of Hogwarts.

We smiled and left the room. Once outside, DK took out his mobile phone from his pocket, like always, and got to booking a cab, in which we would sit silently on either ends of the seat and pretend like we are invisible to each other. And that's why the whole marriage counsellor thing happened.

'Don't book a cab,' I said.

DK looked at me, puzzled.

'Can we walk home instead?'

'That's like an hour's walk from here,' he said, an eyebrow raised quizzically.

'Can we? Please?' I persisted.

DK didn't say anything but placed his mobile phone back in his pocket and started walking towards the exit.

I followed him out on to the footpath.

We started walking. No holding each other's hands or smiling at each other. We didn't talk for what seemed like ten minutes. We just walked. Silently.

People make all kinds of new-year resolutions, don't they? I'd made a few too. And the most important of them was to go out on a dinner date with DK and talk and smile. Like normal couples do. But four months into the new year, we were going to counselling sessions. Dinner dates? Never mind.

I glanced at DK. The frown on his face was still there.

I sighed.

'Remember the day we first met?' I asked him. This is what Anitha had told us to do, right? And this is what we both always avoided talking about.

DK looked at me and hesitantly said, 'Hmm, yeah. Why?' His brow seemed a little less furrowed.

'Remember how scared you were?'

'I wasn't scared, alright?'

'You weren't?' I smiled.

'Okay! I was,' DK agreed. 'And who isn't scared on their first day in a new school, eh? I was sitting alone in the canteen and . . .'

'And that's when I came and sat beside you,' I said, cutting him off.

'Yeah, I remember. You came to me with your two long plaits and this really innocent and cute expression on your face.'

'I was scared too. I mean, boarding schools, by default, are scary. I was scared and I was hoping I would find friends, and then I saw you sitting alone, nervous, and I thought I'd found one.'

'Well, you did,' he said, and seeing a smile on my lips, asked, 'You did, didn't you?'

I smiled.

'What happened?' he asked.

Still smiling, I said, 'Remember what you told me when I asked you your name?'

'Don't,' DK said. 'Don't go there.'

I laughed and imitated him, 'Hi. I am DK'

'Please, yaar. You would do the same if your name was Dilkush Kulkarni.'

'Okay, Dilkush Kulkarni. Sorry!' I mocked.

We broke into laughter in the middle of the road. The moon was now visible in the pale orange glow of the evening sky and the traffic was now building up, along with the honking. The evening bazaar was slowly coming to life. People were crossing the road, a few with their heads bowed over their mobile screens. Some smoked a cigarette right under the no-smoking sign. And among a zillion other people going about their business were a wife and her spouse reminiscing about their good old days, as advised by their counsellor.

'Weren't those days beautiful?' DK asked.

I nodded.

'You didn't talk to me for quite a few days after that day in the canteen,' I reminded him.

He was silent. I looked at him questioningly.

'Hmm . . .'

'Ahem?' I cleared my throat.

'Well, okay!' he said, avoiding my gaze. 'You know how things work in a hostel, don't you?'

'What's that supposed to mean?'

'You know, apparently one of our seniors saw us in the canteen. Later that day, in the hostel, he called me to his room and asked me to stay away from you.'

'Really? You never told me this. Who was this senior?'

'I would rather choose to not say the name of the senior who had a crush on my wife,' he said teasingly.

Was he flirting? Wow!

'Okay, Mr Husband!' I grinned.

He shrugged.

'So then why did you start talking to me again?'

'Because you were persistently trying to talk to me and I felt guilty about ignoring you—and you were sweet too. So, yeah . . .'

Anitha, this is working. He called me sweet!

'You know, Aditi?' DK started, 'I never said this to you and maybe I should have said this to you earlier, but I didn't want to be called desperate or something.'

'What is it?'

'That first day in the canteen, when I saw you, I felt a connection between us. I mean, there were so many other newcomers, but then only you came and sat with me. I know it sounds silly, but for a nervous fifteen-year-old boy, this is a legit reason to feel special about a girl.'

'No, it doesn't sound silly, because, strange as it sounds,' I sighed, 'fifteen-year-old girls have similar feelings too.'

He stopped walking and looked at me. I looked back at him.

Okay, this was really working.

'I am sorry, I guess,' he said, running his fingers through his hair.

We resumed walking. He held my hand. Our fingers interlaced. Our arms touched. This was equally strange and beautiful. We had never talked this way after our marriage. This was like a romantic walk on a pilgrimage of love.

'Do you remember when you got caught that one time?' I asked him.

'When?'

'When you sneaked into the girls' hostel?'

'I wanted to surprise you on your birthday,' he said, after thinking for a minute.

'And our warden surprised you before you could surprise me!'

He laughed, and I laughed too. It is strange, isn't it? How a couple finds certain things funny, which others would not even bat an eyelid for?

'You know, Aditi,' DK started, 'I lost count of the times I did the FLAMES test with our names.'

'Really? What did you get?'

'I don't remember,' he said. 'And, honestly, it doesn't matter, does it? I mean, when you are doing the FLAMES test, something inside you tells you what you want the result to be. I wanted the result to be love. I wanted it to show marriage too. And friendship as well. I know it sounds silly but it made me so happy just to link our names together.'

A smile spread across my face.

'Then why didn't you ask me out on a date?' I asked, trying to not show my silly smile.

'Well, I didn't know how you felt about me and we were fifteen-year-olds then, and I didn't even know if fifteen-year-olds went on date.'

I laughed. Yes, he was innocent back then. He still was.

'But you did take me out, didn't you?'

'Hmm . . . To the Hanuman temple near our school.'

'DK, really? Who takes a girl he loves, or thinks he loves, to a temple? That, too, a Hanuman temple!' I teased.

'I told you,' he said, 'I didn't know what to do. But I knew that I liked being with you and talking to you. And . . .'

He paused.

'And?' I asked.

'And before I realized you were special,' he said coldly, 'you left school, and everything was so confusing thereafter. I think I didn't talk to anybody for days. I didn't know if I'd lost someone I loved, but I knew I'd definitely lost a friend—my only friend—and that disturbed me. Angered me.'

'But I tried calling you—'

DK cut me off. 'I didn't answer your calls,' DK said, looking up at the moon. 'I guess I was angry with you and after a few days you stopped calling, and I tried to forget you and I think I did.'

He sighed.

'Dil, I didn't know what was happening. My father got promoted. He decided to send me to a better school. I missed you. I did. No one at the new school looked at me the way you did. Or whose jokes were as lame as yours. How I hoped for you to take my calls. How badly I wanted to talk with you, Dil.'

DK stopped walking. He pulled me to him and teasingly said, 'Did you just start calling me "Dil"?'

'I did. And this is how I intend to call you from now,' I said with an air of authority.

He laughed and obliged, 'Okay, madam.'

'And then fate gave me a second chance,' DK continued, as he looked at me. 'Gave us a second chance. When my mom, out of the blue, showed me your picture last year and asked if I was ready for marriage. I didn't answer for days.'

DK softly continued, 'All the confusion that I'd tried to forget returned and brought the forgotten anger with it. But I was happy because I saw your picture after years. My parents didn't know you were once a very special friend to me. They didn't even know I once took you to a Hanuman temple for a date. Was that a game chance was playing with us, Aditi? I don't know. But, eventually, I told them that I wanted to marry you. Because that was what I wanted.'

'When my dad showed me your picture,' I said, 'I . . . I was happy too.'

He paused, turned to me, held my hands and said, 'Listen, Aditi . . . I know I messed up, okay? And I am sorry. I think it was the anger that you, my only friend, had left me alone when I didn't have anyone else to talk with that made me sulk all this time. That stopped me from telling you how tasty the food you cook is and how beautiful you are and how deeply I love you. I think that I knew it all this while but I didn't want to accept it. But now, Aditi, I think we don't need Anita's help any more. We will work things out—together. I mean, look, you are with me now and I loved you. I still love you. And I think you love me too.'

He looked at me, waiting for a response.

'Of course I love you, Dil.' I said. 'I have been waiting for a year for you to tell me this.' I stepped closer to embrace him.

We hugged for I don't know how long. It felt as if time had stopped, like it happens in the movies. It was magical.

The crescent moon hung high above our heads. The clouds covered the stars. A street vendor was frying fresh fish on the other side of the road. Hadn't I wanted to go on a dinner date with DK?

'I want to eat that fish fry,' I told him, pointing across the road.

He looked in the direction I'd pointed in and said, 'It's not healthy.'

How typical of him!

'I want it. Please!'

He sighed. 'You do realize that you are cute when you do this, don't you?'

With this, he turned and crossed the road. Once he reached the fish-fry vendor, he turned to me and signalled that it would take five minutes. I nodded. I wanted to eat it with him. Our first dinner date. A romantic roadside fish-fry date.

After five minutes, he turned around with two plates, one in each hand. And started crossing the road. I could see his face glowing. I could feel that he was equally excited. He climbed the divider and jumped down. I was already making plans for when we got home—the playlist we would have on while we danced, the way we would contradict each other's *Harry Potter* theories while gazing at

the stars, with our backs against our balcony wall, and laugh
and maybe kiss too, with the bracing night breeze whistling
around us. DK raised his left arm to wipe the sweat off his
forehead. A car honked.

I looked to the left. 'D-I-L!' I screamed, my eyes wide
with fear. I was sweating and my heart was pounding. The
car sped towards DK. The two plates he was carrying fell
to the floor, its contents strewn. I screamed his name again.

DK looked at the car that was now speeding away and
mumbled something under his breath. It had missed him
by inches. He got up and came rushing to me, and hugged
me tight. He kept telling me that he was all right, but my
heart was beating too fast to respond. My mind was numb.
He kissed my forehead. And at that moment I knew that I
loved him. And he knew it too.

After what seemed like an eternity, we started walking
again. In silence. He put his arm around my shoulder, glad
that fate hadn't let the car separate us. Again.

Inches. It had missed DK by inches. But what if . . . ?
I didn't want to know.

I took my mobile phone out and texted Anitha:
'The doors of the closet are now open.'

4

A Cocoon of Love

Ruby Gupta

Mala stretched languorously on the dishevelled bed and grinned joyously. She had not felt this good in years. A long-forgotten feeling of exhilaration coursed through her veins. Impulsively, she jumped out of bed and did a jig, laughing out loud. Whirling around, Mala suddenly caught a glimpse of herself in the mirror. She moved closer and inspected herself.

The animated eyes, full pink lips, flushed cheeks, endearingly tangled tresses, glowing complexion, all seemed to belong to some attractive stranger. Her luminous eyes seemed to contain within them some mysterious, delightful secret. An impish smile of exultation further intensified the beauty of her countenance. She leaned forward and kissed the charming woman in the mirror.

Involuntarily, her mind went back to her wedding night almost a decade ago . . .

Mala was an exquisitely beautiful, coy bride, eagerly awaiting her new, yet-unfamiliar husband. The mandatory wedding night of the countless Hindi movies that she had watched flashed through her mind. She smiled to herself in anticipation.

Of course, her husband was a far cry from the fair, well-fed Hindi-film hero.

'A man is judged by his position and not by his looks,' her mother had admonished her when she had raised the subject after her marriage had been 'arranged'.

'A plain man will love you all the more for your beauty,' her mother had consoled her, softening a little.

And so now she waited, expecting her husband to lovingly and tenderly initiate her into the joys of marital life.

Just then, her husband, Shankar, entered and immediately locked the door, shutting out his numerous relatives who thronged outside, joking among themselves.

Mala shrank within herself.

Shankar moved up to her and lifted her chin. 'You are so beautiful,' he said, smiling gloatingly. 'I'm going to really enjoy being married to you.'

Mala gazed at him with a smile.

'I've hated my colour for as long as I can remember, but I couldn't do anything about it. So I did the next best thing. I got a milky-white bride for myself!' Shankar grinned triumphantly.

Her mother was right, Mala thought to herself. He will really, truly love me for the rest of my life. What more can a woman ask for? So what if he was too tall, too thin and too dark? After all, he was a civil servant and, to top it, was madly in love with her.

'Let me see what you look like.' Shankar reached for her sari.

Alarmed, Mala jerked back.

'Your innocence is really exciting,' he moved closer, oblivious to her trapped expression.

His fingers were upon her sari now. She stared in horrified fascination at the long, large-jointed, bony fingers against the crimson silk.

'Remember, your married life will be hell if you displease your husband on your wedding night,' her mother's words rang incessantly in her mind.

Shankar was sitting so close to her that she could feel his breath on her skin.

A shudder went through her as the image of a furry spider crawling up her untouched body darted through her mind.

'Beautiful . . . really beautiful . . .' murmured Shankar gleefully, as he seemed to drink in her beauty with his lustful eyes.

Much later, as Mala stared at the long snake-like back of her sleeping husband, she was unable to come to terms with what had happened. She had expected Shankar to go into raptures over her beauty, proclaim his undying devotion to her, maybe even say a poem in praise of her. Instead, he had simply violated her. It seemed like a nightmare. But the searing pain was real. Numbly, she looked at the whirring fan overhead, waiting for the agony to subside.

After a while, Mala dragged herself out of bed and stumbled into the bathroom. She bathed vigorously, trying to wash away all traces of her husband.

Later, restlessly tossing and turning, she tried to sleep. But her mind was too agitated. Thoughts of running away plagued her. Had she married an animal? How could Shankar have been so insensitive, so selfish, so callous? Mala had never been treated so badly in her entire life.

The fact that Shankar had utilized her for his gratification in such a coarse, barbarous manner distressed her.

Gradually exercising all her willpower, she calmed down. Consoling herself that in time it would be better, she fell asleep.

But it was not to be. In the early hours of the morning, rude hands woke her up abruptly. And once again she submitted silently to the torture her husband meted out to her.

When, after several weeks of the daily torment, Mala protested, Shankar countered pompously, 'Any other woman would be pleased to get so much attention from me. But you! If it weren't for your beauty, I would never come near a cold woman like you!'

Mala began hating her looks. She wished fervently that she would turn into an ugly hag. Then perhaps she would be spared this daily humiliation by her husband.

One day, when her mother persistently questioned Mala about her constantly sad expression, she broke down and related everything.

'But, my dear, this is the fate of every woman. I had thought that by now you would have learnt to accept it,' her mother counselled.

'But, Maa, I hate it—and I hate him. How can he be so insensitive to my feelings?'

'Stop pitying yourself. You are not the only woman in such a position. It's a wife's duty. Be thankful that he has not strayed but has provided you with everything any woman can ask for. Look at your status as an IAS officer's wife!' her mother's tone hardened.

'Oh Maa! You don't know what it's like . . .' Mala wailed piteously.

Cutting in, her mother retorted, 'I know what it's like. Do you think your father and I live as brother and sister?'

'Maa!' Mala was shocked. 'But Papa is such a tender, loving man,' she protested.

'Isn't Shankar extremely gentle with his nieces and nephews?' her mother countered.

At this, Mala was left speechless, trying to come to terms with her mother's words.

After a while she said, 'But Papa . . . I don't believe it.'

'Believe me, all men are the same,' her mother said bitterly with pursed lips.

So it was, day after day, year after year. It was just as T.S. Eliot had said not so long ago:

> The meal is ended, she is bored and tired,
> Endeavours to engage her in caresses
> Which still are unreproved, if undesired.
> Flushed and decided, he assaults at once;
> Exploring hands encounter no defense;
> His vanity requires no response,
> And makes a welcome of indifference.

Over the years, Mala endeavoured repeatedly to establish a semblance of some kind of friendship with Shankar. But all her efforts came to naught. Shankar was simply not interested in her as a separate human being. For him, she seemed to exist only in her capacity as a beautiful wife to display and for his own pleasure. She was supposed to be a useful extension to himself. Her role was to smoothly run his home and be an exemplary hostess to his relatives, friends, colleagues and acquaintances. And, of course, cater to his needs in the bedroom. Apart from that, there was nothing that Shankar wanted to do with her.

Shankar never talked to her—really talked to her—about anything. There was no friendship, no camaraderie, no companionship. All their conversations were perfunctory, related to whatever he needed her to do for him. There was only the mundane that they ever talked about. There was nothing of the profound or the sublime or the intellectual in their talks—ever. There was no fun-filled repartee or light-hearted banter either.

After years of futile attempts, entreaties, tears, cajoling and begging, Mala gave up trying to establish a deeper connection with her husband. She withdrew further into a shell. She began existing at a superficial level, while the real Mala disappeared—bit by bit, and then completely.

With the passage of time and the birth of two children, Mala indeed lost all her charm and vitality. She always looked pale, depressed and her mouth perpetually drooped.

Yet her sharp features and fair colour remained . . . And Shankar still did not stray . . .

Then Ketaki entered her life. The smart, savvy, unflappably cool Ketaki ran her own garment export unit. They hit it off at their very first meeting and, in an incredibly short time, became very close friends. Ketaki was everything that Mala had ever wanted to be. Ketaki, on the other hand, was drawn to the vulnerable softness that enveloped Mala like a mist. Somehow, it seemed but natural that they exchanged their innermost secrets.

Ketaki had never married, being put off men after seeing her hard-working mother abused every day by her unemployed, alcoholic, brutish father. She was further alienated from the male species when a cousin whom she had looked up to molested her. Ketaki had vowed that she would never allow any man to gain control over her in any way—least of all her heart.

Mala could not help but admire the manner in which Ketaki had taken charge of her life. By now they had started meeting every day for lunch. At times they giggled like schoolgirls and, at others, exchanged their pain and anguish.

At last Mala had found someone who understood and empathized with her. They shared the same interests and had a similar outlook towards life.

Slowly Mala became infected with Ketaki's verve and energy. She seemed to flower for the first time in her life, while Ketaki lost some of her tough businesswoman facade and smiled more often.

Ketaki urged Mala to get back her individuality, her identity. Mala did not even know what that was.

'Think back. What did you love doing most in school, in college? There must have been something,' Ketaki coaxed fervently.

'Er . . . it . . . it was oil painting . . .' Mala spoke diffidently.

'Well, there you have it. You are going to become a painter!'

Brushing aside all of Mala's protestations, Ketaki hauled her to the market and bought her easels, paints, brushes and all the paraphernalia needed for painting.

'But what will Shankar say? Will he allow it?' Mala was apprehensive.

'Nonsense. You just need to be smart about it. You have to present this to Shankar as another feather in your cap.'

'Meaning?' Mala was confused.

'Meaning Shankar would be all too glad to show off to the world that his trophy wife is not only gorgeous but an artist too.'

'Er . . . do you think it will work?' Mala was hesitant.

'Of course! I know exactly how men like Shankar think. Just do as I say.' Ketaki was confident.

Mala nodded. Her being began to fill with a long-forgotten excitement at the thought of using the paintbrush after years.

'Now the first thing you do is convert one of the guest rooms of your sprawling bungalow into a studio. After that, all you have to do is paint. Paint like never before. Pour all your angst, all your emotions, everything, into your paintings,' Ketaki spoke passionately.

Mala looked at Ketaki in wonder. Was she a goddess, the thought came to her, and tears almost welled up in her eyes.

A month later, Mala invited Ketaki to her studio when no one was at home. Ketaki went from painting to painting exclaiming in delight. 'This is better than I expected.'

'Really? You really think so?' Mala's art teachers in school and college had always loved her paintings—but that had been so long ago.

'Yes.' Ketaki was firm. 'Now I want you to make about thirty more, in addition to these six, and then we will exhibit them in one of the art galleries.'

Mala was speechless. For the first time in her life, she began to dream . . .

To Mala, Ketaki was everything she never had. She was her mentor, her best friend, her brother, sister, girlfriend, boyfriend, buddy, doting mother, indulgent father, partner-in-crime, confidante—everything. Bit by bit, Ketaki began filling the painful void—the humungous aching crater within her that had swallowed up the real Mala eons ago.

They felt like long-lost soulmates united at last.

One afternoon while sharing their daily lunch, Ketaki said, 'I don't feel like going back to my office. Let's go back to my apartment for a nice siesta.'

'Okay.' Mala was all too ready. In any case, her children returned at six after attending school and subsequent tuition classes. And Shankar returned only by nine or much later.

Later, lying in Ketaki's eclectically designed bedroom and holding hands, they felt at peace.

'This is the first time I've taken time off since I started working,' Ketaki broke the companionable silence.

'And I feel free for the first time in years.' Mala smiled.

'I love your hair.' Ketaki softly caressed Mala's silky locks.

'Hmm . . . that feels so good!' Mala purred languidly as a heavy lassitude overcame her limbs. Her eyes grew heavy and a contented smile curved her mouth. It seemed the most natural thing in the world to pull Ketaki into her arms. Ketaki's arms embraced her tenderly. Mala experienced gentle vibes enveloping her. From somewhere deep within her, copious tears started flowing down her cheeks and heavy sobs racked her, as years of anger, sorrow and frustration rolled out of her. The calm that followed left her with only one deep feeling—of being loved and cared for as never before.

Holding Ketaki close, she whispered, 'I love you, I love you, I love you . . .'

'I know. I love you too,' cooed Ketaki.

The hours passed in sheer bliss. At last Mala understood the ramifications of her own being. Finally she had become true to herself. She was complete now.

In the ten years of marriage, Mala had never formed any kind of attachment with Shankar. Whereas here, within a few hours, a lifelong irrevocable bond had been formed.

Ketaki emerged from the kitchen with two steaming cups of tea, and Mala was brought back from her ruminations. They smiled at each other mischievously, sipping their tea in silence. Words were unnecessary, for they knew that each belonged to the other in an immutable union. Till now their lives had been like a parched desert, but at last they had been blessed with the nourishing rain of love and life. This was their own cocoon of love, which no one in the world could breach. And as evening fell, they left the apartment, hand in hand, towards their separate destinations, with joy in their hearts and a spring in their step.

5

The Matchmaker

Anuj Dutt

It was winter and I was sitting in the lawn waiting for the school bus to drop my daughter Amaira home. The bus came and the little lady got off. When she saw me she came running. I was really proud of my fifteen-year-old.

'I am going to be Samyukta, and Rohan will be Prithviraj Chauhan!' she shouted before breaking into her favourite jig. Well, she had landed the role she wanted in her school play, Chand Bardai's *Prithviraj Raso*. For me it was a dazzling tale of medieval romance. However, I knew that the authenticity of the Samyukta episode was in history's grey area of sorts.

The legend is that Samyukta, the headstrong princess of Kannauj, and Prithviraj Chauhan, a Rajput king, fell deeply in love. On finding out about the love affair, Raja Jaichand, who was Samyukta's father and the king of Kannauj, was livid that a romance had been blossoming without his knowledge and that, too, with a king he could not stand. Jaichand decided to insult Prithviraj and arranged a swayamvara for his daughter, an event where she would garland a husband of her choice from a galaxy of invited royalty. Prithviraj was, of course, not invited. To insult him further, Jaichand commissioned a clay statue of Prithviraj in the form of a lowly guard of his court and installed it at the entrance.

Prithviraj, on hearing about the ceremony, devised a plan. Now there are two versions of how things went after that. One version says that Prithviraj hid *behind the statue* and another says that he *removed the statue* the night before and stood in its place. On the day of the ceremony, Samyukta walked through the court holding the ceremonial garland. Ignoring the gaze of her ardent suitors, she passed through the door and put the garland around the neck of Prithviraj's statue. The 'statue' magically came to life, sweeping Samyukta off her feet, literally, setting her on his horse and riding away with her to Delhi, his kingdom. Till date, I believe this is what a true swashbuckling romance is about!

Coming back to the present, as per the deal struck with Amaira a few days back, it was agreed that if she landed the role, I would narrate to her and her little sister, Naina, how I'd won my 'Samyukta'! They knew patches of how Rekha, their mother, and I got married. My in-laws and my parents had strictly censored the uncomfortable bits and had told them their own versions. I wanted both my children to hit their teens before I could share the true chain of events that had transpired so many years ago.

After dinner, we were all to curl up on the sofa for the grand narration. I had serious doubts about my storytelling skills. While revising the narrative in my head, I recalled how, in those days, the messengers of romance were PCO and STD booths, and how, for arranged marriages, the girl's photo was sent to the boy's by speed post and a pre-arranged match under intensive parental supervision was the done thing. And I wondered if I would come out at the end of the narration as dashing as the Prithviraj Chauhan of history lessons. In the world that Amaira and Naina lived in, mobile phones had replaced STD booths, and it was not just the girl's photo that was sent any more, it was the boy's too—for which they used WhatsApp and email. And meetings took place in one of the numerous coffee shops that had sprung up, of course after their respective profiles were vetted on LinkedIn, Instagram and Facebook.

After dinner, I was called to the living-room sofa. Both Amaira and Naina had worked on the setting—a dim lamp in the corner and soft Kenny G music coming from the speakers. I was nervous.

I told myself that in the story I was about to narrate, I had won—fair and square—and that I was very proud of my victory. And unlike Prithviraj Chauhan's story with Samyukta, which was supposedly pure fiction, I had over a dozen friends and relatives who had witnessed my amazing win. On top of that, I had two wonderful daughters and a soulmate of nineteen years to show for it.

I sat down, cleared my throat and began my story:

This isn't a tale about people living together peacefully in a small residential colony. It is not a story that has a lesson to be learnt at the end. It is a story about how I won your mother from the matchmaker.

The place where this story takes place is a peaceful neighbourhood. Back when it happened, it was a place where bureaucrats during their service years bought small plots and constructed their retirement havens. A mini kingdom for all the retired subjects of 'babudom'. Their children stayed with them. Some of the children left for jobs or higher studies elsewhere. Some, like me, waited for their fathers to pull the right strings and press the right buttons to get jobs. It was an easy life. We were a pretty big group of eleven guys, to start with, but slowly our group grew smaller as our fathers found the right connections that made things work for us and got us jobs.

This was at a time when about five of us were waiting for one of those 'we have a post just for you' calls. To pass time we would play chess and carom at each other's homes from about five in the evening to about seven. And then it was off to the local market to meet Ruchi, Rekha and Rohini.

After all, we were young men with hearts. Three of us had our soulmates identified. The other two were still searching. And, no, the three R's were not sisters. There was talk of marriage, of undying love—all hidden from parents, of course. But we were all sensible people, who wanted good pay packets before dowries.

Then came the matchmaker.

As I have already said, people who retired came to settle in our colony. So did the matchmaker—Mr Shastri, a widower. Having retired from some obscure department somewhere deep in the state secretariat, he'd come to spend the rest of his life in our peaceful colony. At the very beginning he gave us the idea that he was there just to do some gardening and play a round of rummy every now and then. It was the rummy that started all the trouble. From the terrace of one of my friends, Anil, we would see this man in a kurta pyjama and a brown blazer walking towards Mr Sanyal's house. Mr Sanyal was Rohini's father. And Anil was in love with Rohini.

Mr Shastri, in one of the rummy sessions, mentioned a close friend of his in Lucknow whose son worked in Germany as an engineer. He would be the perfect match for Rohini. Would the Sanyals be interested?

The Sanyals were, of course, very interested! STD calls were made and a postcard-size colour photograph of Rohini—taken some months ago for this very purpose— was sent by speed post to Lucknow. The reply, too, came by speed post. The match was made and accepted. A month later, Rohini Mitra, née Sanyal, left for Germany.

Anil first contemplated suicide; then came Ghalib, followed by vodka. Vodka, because that was the only bottle left in his father's liquor cabinet. But within a month he was back to his normal self. A few weeks later, he got that lucky phone call and was off to Mumbai to work for a big MNC.

Mr Shastri, who had received a lot of fame in our neighbourhood for fixing such a good match, was well rewarded—a gold wristwatch from the bride's family and a Mont Blanc pen set from the groom's. However, I think it was the fame that spurred him on. The kind of fame that he must have always dreamt of achieving while working for the government, but which had always eluded him. He went on to arrange more matches.

Preeti, the daughter of Mr Gupta, was married off to a chartered accountant from Chennai. The chartered accountant was the son of another of Mr Shastri's friends. He was obviously well rewarded here as well, because a few days later we saw him on a shiny new moped. And then he turned his attention to Ruchi, Shekhar's sweetheart. This time the match came from England. Shekhar tried to convince Ruchi to elope but she was swept off her feet by the lad from London. I enjoyed all this because I knew Rekha was devoted to me, and a job for me was not far. I knew Rekha would wait, but would your grandparents? They wanted a match for her from any country that was a member of the United Nations and carried a passport that did not have the Ashoka emblem on it.

Mr Shastri began his search; I began to prepare for war.

Rekha and I couldn't talk to each other any more as your grandfather began to accompany her on her trips to the market. My friends told me to give up. But I struggled on. I decided to vent my frustrations on anything that reminded me of Mr Shastri. On Sunday mornings I would join Pinto, my dog, in ripping apart the matrimonial columns of the newspaper. One dark night I punctured the tyre of the moped. I threw rocks at his windowpanes. And as if to spite me, a few days later, he brought a match for Rekha—a doctor from Australia. He didn't know about her and me. I wondered what he would have done if he had.

So now the groom's family were to come to see your mother soon. I had a plan. I was desperate, and so the rumours started. It was in the market that I saw them both talking—Mrs Prasad and the matchmaker. I came home and set the wheels rolling. I told your dadi how I had seen them together at so many parks, cinemas and restaurants. What was happening to good old middle-class morality? It was a plain lie with not an ounce of truth to it. Mr Prasad was an alcoholic and Mrs Prasad a devoted wife. But the die had been cast. Thanks to your grandmother and her loyal maidservant, the rumour spread.

Suddenly people did not want to play rummy with the matchmaker any more. He received no more invites to any tea or dinner parties, and people began to avoid him at the market. And your mother's parents were also not interested in this lover avatar of the matchmaker. They made it clear that they would join the matchmaker's social boycott—but only after their daughter's marriage.

I was in a hopeless situation. My sweetheart was about to become part of India's beauty drain.

I was alone at home that day when the bell rang. It was the matchmaker. Over the past few weeks he seemed to have aged quite a bit. He walked in. I told him that my parents were not at home.

'I want to talk to you,' he said. 'You love Rekha?'

I nodded.

'So it was you who was behind the broken windowpanes, the deflated tyres, the obscene phone calls and, of course, the rumours.'

So he had found out, from God knows where. I remained calm. He had dark circles under his eyes. Sleep, it seemed, had eluded him for a long time. Served him right. But I was still overcome with pity. We were sitting in the drawing room. I offered him a glass of water.

'The rumours must stop. Think about the lady, at least. That husband of hers is an alcoholic; he has started hitting her. Your prank has snowballed into something bigger—or should I say . . . revenge.'

His words hit me like arrows. If he had expected me to break down and beg for his forgiveness, he was expecting too much. But the fact is I did.

He comforted me. 'It's okay. Love makes people do strange things.'

I tried my best to stop those rumours. It took about eight months. Rekha's wedding with the doctor Mr Shastri had suggested never took place. Mr Shastri told the groom's family to make some outrageous dowry demands. The result was that your Nana (grandfather) threw them out of the house. And it was Mr Shastri who did all this for me. I think he did forgive me.

I married your mother a year later.

A week after my wedding, Mr Shastri, along with Mrs Prasad, disappeared from the colony. They are now rumoured to be living together happily in Delhi.

I looked at my two daughters, awaiting their verdict. I had impressed myself immensely with my storytelling skills and felt like Prithviraj Chauhan in his full battle regalia, armour glinting in the sun, chest puffed up.

'Well, what do you think?' I asked.

Naina was the first to remark. 'You actually cried when Mr Shastri came to meet you?'

That's why daughters are special—a father crying is a big deal for them.

And somewhere the spirit of Prithviraj smiled.

6

Destiny Swipes Right

Rachita Ramya

Vaishnavi

Buzz!

I felt my phone vibrate on my mattress, indicating another notification from the new guy I had been speaking to for the past twenty minutes. These dating apps were the new way of connecting with people these days. I would be missing out on all these single guys if I wasn't registered on them. My friend and roommate Sunita had warned me that most of these apps had creeps hiding behind their profiles, demanding all sorts of crazy things from girls. But Sunita was a pessimist. I mean, she accused dolphins of being emotionless sex addicts. Cute, innocent, smiling dolphins!

So it was no surprise that men as a species fared quite poorly in her eyes.

'Not all men are bad, Sunita.' I would roll my eyes at her, annoyed.

But men had proven me wrong—time and time again. This was my last attempt at online dating now.

Although this new guy I was talking to did seem really nice. We hadn't talked for that long, but I could tell he—

'Are you busty?'

—he was just like the rest of them!

I was done. I furiously tapped my fingers on my phone and deleted the app before my dating horror story could worsen.

I was giving up. Finding your soulmate was harder than I had anticipated.

Being Indian, it was assumed that I would always have the option of arranged marriage open to me, but my parents were the last people I would trust to find me a guy. For all I knew, they would find the most convenient, accessible guy who would be willing to 'settle' for their daughter, and then spend the rest of their unexpended energy convincing me that he was the one.

No, thank you. Almost six years back, when I had stepped out of my hometown in Punjab and flown to Mumbai, I had sworn I would be leading my life on my terms. This was *my* dream life.

Having said that, being ghosted and friend-zoned by the guys in the dating world was not the dream I had anticipated. The dating scene in Mumbai was hell for someone like me. Being the nerd that I was, I hadn't played any actual games—and now I was required to play all these manipulative dating games.

Text only after three days of meeting someone.

When interested, act like you are not interested.

Don't mention you are looking for anything serious too early into the relationship.

These rules were harder to remember than BODMAS in math equations. Needless to say, I was a math geek trying to survive in a world where the laws of logic did not apply.

'I am never going to find anyone, Sunita. I am going be single forever,' I stated when I met her for coffee near our apartment.

'Join the club!' Sunita said exuberantly.

'This is nothing to be happy about,' I grumbled.

Somehow, we had exchanged roles in this conversation. Right now I was the pessimist.

'How are things with new guy? The one whose profile you saw and mentally decided you are going to marry him before even sending him a "hi"?'

There were times I wished I could kill Sunita. Now was one of those times. But she was partially right. I was super picky about these guys on the dating apps. And, somehow, I still always picked the wrong ones.

'He turned out just like the rest of them,' I muttered under my breath.

'Well, no wonder! You met him on Hickie. That's a hook-up app. Everyone knows that!'

I gaped at her.

'You recommended it to me!'

'Yeah, for fooling around and letting your hair down before finding someone worthwhile. I never told you to expect to find your soulmate there,' Sunita told me in the 'I told you so' tone she reserved only for me. 'If you want a more civilized app for settling down with someone, try this new app called Beloved. People get married after meeting there.'

'You told me two of your friends got married after meeting on Hickie.'

'Yes . . . these were other friends . . . who got married after hooking up on Hickie.' Sunita hesitated, trying to hide her guilt. 'But you, with your Indian values, don't believe in hooking up, right?'

I gave her a frustrated look.

Although it had nothing to do with Indian values, I didn't believe in the casual dating culture that had taken over the world. I was looking for something *real*.

'Anyway, let's forget this for now and go out. It's Saturday night!' Sunita changed the topic just as we were about to finish our café lattes.

I nodded. I guess getting lost in a crowd of people at a club was a good way to forget your loneliness.

After we came back home to get ready, I sat in silence in my room. I hated the empty feeling of being alone in a big city like Mumbai. I wanted someone to be there for me.

I grabbed my phone and browsed Instagram for something to cheer me up.

No luck. Just happy couples going on vacays, nowhere close to mirroring my anxiety. These days Instagram was a trigger for me to feel depressed. Truth was, I was alone. And it scared me more than anything else in the world.

'Let's go!' Sunita's booming voice came from outside.

I scanned myself in the mirror. I looked underdressed for a Saturday night in the city. No make-up, simple clothes, long hair swept back in a messy ponytail. I also had my spectacles on, giving the impression of being dressed for a casual Sunday.

I don't care, I said to myself, slamming the door behind me.

Karan

The Saturday-night scene in Mumbai was like a celebration of the epic 'work hard, party harder' saying. My friends had dragged me to this brand-new club that had recently opened in south Mumbai. The sparkling, shiny crowd of decked-up girls was hard to ignore, but here I was, looking at my phone for the hundredth time. The girl I had been speaking to on this app had gone AWOL. My mistake completely. I was not paying attention while typing and autocorrect decided to change my words from harmless to sexually elaborate. Even offensive.

I tried to hide my laughter. This was really a funny situation and if that girl had just waited a few minutes for me to apologize, we could have been on a date now, laughing about the incident together.

I shook my head. *Girls these days.*

Suddenly, my eyes stopped at this girl who had decided to come into the glamorous club dressed as . . . herself. This was refreshing to see.

She looked familiar. I wondered if we had bumped into each other before.

'Hi,' I smiled at her.

Her hazel-brown eyes widened. Did we know each other from somewhere?

'The app,' she said as if she had read my mind.

So I had already met her in the virtual world.

This was the same girl from Hickie, the one who had been offended by autocorrect on my phone.

In the warped real–virtual dichotomy, it was hard to imagine that behind the picture on these apps was a walking, talking, breathing, *real* person. But looking at her dimple deepen in her cheeks as she flashed me a gorgeous smile was confirmation that she was, in fact, real. And right now she was barely standing a few inches from me.

'Oh yeah! Vaishnavi! You look different in person. Good different,' I emphasized.

She did not look like the dolled-up girl from her profile.

Glancing at her horn-rimmed glasses, I wondered if she was a closet geek like me. That would be so cool.

I also noticed we had a pretty significant height difference. And she hadn't attempted to conceal her height by wearing extra inches of heels, unlike the rest of the girls at the club.

'You look great too,' she replied, looking up at me.

Had she blushed a little when she said that, or was that my imagination?

These party clubs, with their over-the-top music and neon blinking lights, seemed to have psychedelic powers that could almost play with your head.

I could see her friend was trying to nudge her into a private gossip session.

'Well, if you are *busy* now, we can catch up later.' I winked at her and hoped that she would forgive me for my mistake earlier. Or, rather, excuse my phone's mistake.

As she looked at me with a surprised expression on her face, I realized it must have finally dawned on her.

'Oh, so you meant *busy* earlier! I just thought . . . actually, I just thought . . .'

' . . . That I am a creep,' I finished her sentence. 'It was a typo, but you were quick to judge me, like I was quick to judge you. I thought you were this really glamorous, high-maintenance girl.'

'I am anything but that,' she said, a little defensively.

'Yes, she is not high-maintenance at all!' her friend chimed in.

'It's really nice to meet you in person,' I said, looking into Vaishnavi's eyes meaningfully, hoping she would get the hint.

I did like her, a little more than normal. Her heart-shaped face was hard to ignore. She stood out even when she clearly wasn't trying to.

As we continued staring at each other, I realized maybe this was meant to happen. Otherwise why else, in a city of about eighteen million, would two people run into each other twice on the same day?

'Could you excuse us for just a second?' her friend decided to interrupt again.

'Sure.'

What was it about girls talking to their best friends about everything?

She whispered something into Vaishnavi's ears while I tried not to eavesdrop.

'We will just be back,' Vaishnavi said with an expression that was hard to read.

They disappeared into the crowd and I was left wondering if I had done something wrong again.

The DJ was finally in the house and in a matter of seconds, the club walls started thumping with Bollywood pop remixes. I could see the dance floor was lit with a crowd of people determined to break a leg. I hoped it would be their own.

I looked at my watch. It had been fifteen minutes since Vaishnavi and her friend had been gone. There was a strong possibility that they weren't coming back.

'Hey! We are all going to this other club in Bandra. Do you want to tag along?' One of my friends shouted at me over the unbearably loud music.

'No, you guys go. I will just go home now.'

It had been a long day. And, most probably, I had been stood up by the same girl twice—on an app and now in person.

I hated this millennial culture. I was done.

Never again was I going to rely on these dating apps to meet my soulmate.

Vaishnavi

Last night, because of Sunita, I had managed to lose the guy from the app. By the time we came back with drinks, he was gone. Vanished into the sea of people.

Except it wasn't my intention to lose him this time. Meeting Karan in person had made him more human. And I realized he never meant to make me uncomfortable in our virtual interaction. It was just a silly mistake. One made by his phone's intuitive memory.

I had made the mistake of judging Karan too soon. And after literally being handed a second chance by serendipity, I had lost him again.

Today, I downloaded Hickie again, only to find that he had deleted his profile from the app.

I didn't even know his full name. There were a gazillion Karans on social media. I would never find him.

'I hate you!' I said to Sunita for the umpteenth time. 'Why did you have to convince me to get drinks to loosen up?'

'It wasn't my fault. The line was too long, and the bartender was inexperienced. And I thought your friend would wait for us . . .'

'It's no use discussing this now,' I said, as Karan's handsome face loomed before my eyes. 'He might have gone home with some other girl.'

But even as I said those words, my mind refused to believe that. We had something. A spark. A feeling. A strange kind of chemistry?

My math brain quickly brought me back to the sad reality of logic.

Sparks don't last a lifetime. Commitments do. And Karan had decided to leave without even saying goodbye. While heroes in famous love stories could wait a lifetime to get a glimpse of their lady love, Karan hadn't even cared enough to wait fifteen minutes.

'Maybe it wasn't meant to be,' I announced with a heavy heart.

'Listen, don't feel bad. There are plenty of guys in Mumbai and—'

'—and none for me to date,' I groaned.

'No! That's not true!' Sunita, the reformed optimist, urged. 'Wait, let's get you on Beloved.'

After one hour of vehemently refusing, I finally let her create my profile on Beloved.

I was still unsure about this. Were people really that replaceable in this new era of dating?

'Voila!' she exclaimed as she signed in with my social media account. 'Now let's find your soulmate.'

I looked at the profiles, feeling dejected for some reason.

Why couldn't I have asked for Karan's phone number? Or his full name?

These new men were all good-looking, but I felt I had shared something special with Karan. Something intangible. Maybe it was just a spark, but I wanted to explore more.

'I think I want to go off this app, Sunita.'

I instinctively decided to pull the plug on this online dating thing.

'But at least look at some of them . . .'

'I don't want to look at anyone,' I said stubbornly as I tried to snatch my phone from her hands.

But just as I wriggled to free my phone from Sunita's claw-like grasp, her fingers swiped to the next profile by mistake.

And I saw the face I had been seeking.

Dressed in a grey T-shirt and black shorts, he was standing in the middle of what looked like Juhu beach. His face was partially covered with a pair of Ray–Ban sunglasses, but I could still see his lopsided grin. The one that had made me want to meet him in person. The grin that had melted my heart when I had actually met him in person.

'Isn't this the same guy?' Sunita asked in surprise.

I stared at his picture in disbelief.

There come moments in life when people get exactly what they have asked for and they don't know how to deal with it. Sometimes, in these moments, confusion precedes joy.

I played around with his picture smiling up at me—*left, right, left . . .?*

'There,' Sunita announced as she swiped right for me, relieving me of my anxiety. 'Maybe it *is* meant to be.'

Or not. His profile had been marked inactive.

I would find out soon enough.

But after hours of frantically checking my phone, I realized there was a possibility of never hearing from Karan.

I looked at my phone again, hoping something had changed in the last thirty seconds.

And, sure enough, there was a notification.

7

Love Transcends Generations

Rupali Tiwari

I am sitting in front of my granddaughter. She is crying but I can't hear her. Maybe because my hearing has faded with age or maybe because she doesn't have the strength to cry loudly.

Since when have we become so powerless that all we can do is watch our children cry?

'Darling,' I say, putting my hand on her head, 'if you won't tell me what the matter is, how will I help you?'

She looks up at me with red eyes. She must have been crying for a long time. She coughs, dries her eyes with her hands and smears her kajal and the other gooey thing girls put on their eyes these days. In my days, it was just kajal and that, too, in a brass container, made from the smoke of earthen diyas.

I wipe her eyes with my sari's pallu. That is what we are supposed to use it for. To wipe our loved ones' tears.

Girls nowadays have no interest in learning how to wear saris or even bother with suits or dupattas. All of them wear jeans or short dresses—our culture going down the drain while we watch.

I watch as my granddaughter gets tired of crying.

'Did someone say something to you?'

She shakes her head.

'Did you fail your exams?'

'I am a content writer, Dadi. I don't go to school any more,' she scoffs.

I smile. Kids these days can cry and still have the strength to belittle their elders.

'It's something else,' she finally says.

I wait for her to continue. But that is all she says.

'Look, Anaya. You need to tell me what the matter is or both of us are sitting here in this room all day.'

I can see the eyes widen. I know how hard it can be for a grandchild to stay shut in an old person's room. It's torture. The smell, the old stories.

'I can't marry Pranay.'

Finally, some success.

'Is that it? You don't like a boy your parents have chosen for you?' I laugh. 'Okay, I will tell your father that you are not interested. Go now, and don't cry any more.'

I go back to my book.

'There is something else . . .' she blurts out.

I put my book down and wait.

'I love someone else.'

I was waiting for it. These kids think they are so smart, always on their phones, chatting and smiling. Even an old woman like me can tell who has an affair and who is going through a break-up. I knew Anaya had a boyfriend. Never knew it was this serious.

'Okay. Call him tomorrow. I will tell your father. We will meet him. I can't promise you anything, but we will meet him.'

I am so clever.

'That's not it,' she mumbles again.

And I wait. Again. Where did we go so wrong with this generation?

'We met in college,' she continues. 'Had the same classes. We clicked instantly. For two years we were best friends. But then we graduated, and I realized that I was in love. And we have been in a relationship since then.'

'Look, Anaya. I agreed to talk to your parents. And that's it. You can't force me to like him just yet. Let's wait and see how it goes. And, remember, caste still matters in this house.'

'It's not that,' she sobs. And now it's a high-pitched, ear-ringing cry.

'Anaya, stop it!' It's tiring to watch her cry like that. 'Just tell me the reason. No beating around the bush.'

I am stern now. And any minute I will be at my worst. I am looking at my cane right at this moment.

'You won't get it,' she replies angrily. 'All you think about is what's wrong with this generation and how lowly our thoughts are. You won't understand a thing.'

She is right. That is what I think. But she is wrong. I will understand.

'I wasn't always like this, you know,' I tell her. 'I was like you once. Full of zeal and sparkle. Wanting to do everything on my own. I remember I wanted to work at an office. But in my days it was impossible. I gave up food and water for three days, after which your grandfather finally agreed to let me be the financial head at his company.'

I smiled.

I could have had anything I wanted. I was pretty too. Now I am old and wrinkly. The reason I don't have mirrors in my room.

'It's not that simple, Dadi . . .' She puts her head down on the bed. 'It's more complicated than fighting for a job.'

'Oh, for God's sake, Anaya! Stop with this whining. It's just a boy. Did I raise you so weak that you would cry over a boy?'

'That is the reason you won't understand. Because you are too strict and too conservative!' she shouts. 'I can't believe I came to you for help. Someone who has never been in love will never understand what I am going through.'

Her eyes are flashing with anger.

'Love. I was in love once. We met at the office. He was the first person who welcomed me as if he were welcoming another employee. Just smiled and said not to listen to anyone.'

My husband was not the type of person to show affection. Of course, he had a family to look after and he forgot how to show empathy to his own wife. There was just a marriage between us. We were two people sharing a bed. But love was not required to get married back then.

'I always thought that I fell for Somil, even though I was married, because I didn't like my husband. But now that I am old, I realize that love is not simple to understand. It was so easy for me to fall for Somil. Soon, we started meeting in secret. I didn't even think of the consequences it would have for my three-year-old marriage. I was just too much in love to think. Is that what love is? It makes you someone else. It makes you brave. Well, my bravery flew out the window the day your dada caught me with Somil. For nine months I was meeting Somil until we got caught.'

My granddaughter was listening with her eyes wide.

'I know now love doesn't make you brave, because as soon as I got caught, I denied everything. I denied ever falling for Somil. And said we were just good friends. We didn't do anything. Really. Yes, too boring for this generation, but we weren't raised like that. What I was doing would not be considered cheating nowadays. But back in my days, it was the reason people got divorced. So I just denied everything. I didn't go to the office for a week. And when I returned, Somil was gone. No one could tell me whether he had been fired or if he had just left on his own. After that, love never found me again.'

'Dadi . . .' Anaya taps me. To see whether I am alive or not.

'Yes. And I am not mad at you.' I brush her cheeks softly with my fingers. 'But, darling, you need to tell me the truth.'

'Did you ever think about leaving grandfather?' she asks, head buried in a pillow. Too ashamed to even look at me.

'Yes, I did. After two months, Somil came to me. He asked me to run away with him. He said that we would be happy far away from all this. He said that I was his one true love and that no one else would ever come into his life. I couldn't leave then. I wasn't brave enough. So he left. I didn't see him ever again.'

I look at Anaya. And realize that the love she has been talking about is not that different from what I had felt. But she is different. She has the strength to fight for it.

'Anaya, just trust me. If I like the boy, I will get you married to him,' I say. 'Caste no bar.'

'It's a girl.' She peeps at me from the pillow.

I stare at her. 'What!'

'I love a girl. I want to be with her.'

I am at a loss for words. I can see her crying and staring at me. She looks like a balloon without air. Too empty to rise on its own. She looks deflated. Her greatest secret revealed. She hopes that I will understand. And I do. Love is just that—love.

'Let me and your father meet her. If we like her, then fine. If not, then you will go find yourself another girlfriend. Boy or girl, you will not live with someone who is not right for you.'

For a minute from then, I feel the air squeezed out of my lungs. Anaya is hugging me so tight that I can feel my ribs crushing. Finally, I see her smiling. I can read her eyes. She has been accepted as she is.

This is what love is. It is not about right and wrong. It is about being you and finding the courage to fight for the two of you.

8

Fast Train to Love

Pooja Dubey

She was not fast enough to reach the ladies' coach but enough to catch the train and get into the special coach for people with disabilities. Mumbai trains stop for no one. They follow the schedule strictly and give you only two minutes to find an entry.

She felt somewhat restless even in the nearly empty coach. There were only five people in it—an old blind man, two specially abled women, a young boy and a blind man in his early thirties. She did not belong there.

She had no disability. If a ticket checker caught her, she would have to pay a fine. Local railways staff was very strict and would not take any excuse she offered them. She had to get down at the next station, which was still some distance away, as she had taken a fast train from Mumbai Central, and it would stop next at Dadar.

She did not want to get down at Dadar—it was always super crowded and the mob would crush her if she tried to change the coach. She still remembered the first time she'd boarded a train from Dadar. She had let four trains pass before she could gather the courage to enter one. A person has to be a spirited fighter, willing to throw everyone out of the way to be able to make an entry into a station like Dadar.

So she thought of letting Dadar pass and decided to get down at the next station, Bandra. But she was going to Andheri, which was the station right after Bandra in a fast local. So why not have some more patience and get down directly at her destination? But what if she got caught at Dadar or Bandra? Those ticket checkers acted like undercover agents, blending into the masses in normal clothes. And all of them seemed to have an uncanny eye for defaulters.

If any of them caught her, she decided she would act like she had severe leg pain. After all, she wasn't so bad at acting. Who would examine her leg physically anyway? It was a free country, after all, not like under British rule, when she could have been thrown out brutally. It was only recently that she had seen a short film shared on WhatsApp. It had depicted how their lives could have been if they were still being ruled by the British—a beautiful couple had met with an accident and were treated like shit when they went to a British restaurant to seek shelter and help. She was not committing a crime, so why was this guilt nagging her so much? She could not understand.

She settled down on the last seat in a corner to avoid doubtful stares. The guilt was still large in her head but soon subsided when she saw there were more than enough empty seats for any specially abled person who might get in at Dadar. If more people entered, she anyway had a chance to get down at Bandra, or better still, just stand and give others a chance to sit. Then she wouldn't be wrong, not at least in her own eyes.

Despite so many self-assurances, she could not help but worry and wished she had a panic button she could just switch off. And then she could experience calm. But that wasn't to be.

She wondered how 'Acharya Chanakya', the coach of Samrat Ashoka, could remain so calm even in the most terrifying situations. She had recently seen a few episodes of *Chakravartin Ashoka Samrat* and loved the character of the coach, for he was so intelligent, intuitive and calm. Had he really been like that? Or was it just the exaggeration of a personality? Maybe—how would she ever know? It was not like she could sit in a time machine and go back to the past.

On the opposite bench sat a blind man with black glasses. The glasses looked pretty deluxe. How could a blind man travelling by train afford that, she wondered and kept looking at him. She could not help but notice that his clothes were also expensive. He wore an original grey Zara T-shirt over blue denims. There was also an exquisite watch on his wrist. The man was also healthy, even muscular, and quite handsome. This was strange. She wondered if he was even blind. What if he wasn't? All he had to do was wear dark glasses to look blind. He did not even have a rod that blind people normally carried. But why would a man who could afford riches travel by a cheap train?

'You are wondering if I am blind?' he said in a husky, bold voice.

'What? You can see?' She had not been wrong in her guess. *What a jerk.*

'Yes, I can see, but only partially. I am kind of night-blind. Can't see in the dark.'

'Oh!' She silently scolded herself for being too judgemental, too quickly, and calling him a jerk in her head.

'But you are neither blind nor disabled. Am I right?' he confronted.

'How do you know?'

'You are restless, observing others, conscious, and chose to take the innermost seat despite the empty coach.'

'Maybe I like peace.'

'Really?' He smiled. 'I think you are cautious because you think you might get caught.'

'Wow! You are so observant.'

'Oh, I can be so much more.'

'So much more?'

'I can read minds.'

'Really?' she laughed. 'Trying to impress a girl? Bluffmaster.'

She wondered if he was some kind of a philanderer and this was his pick-up line for women. After all, he was handsome and wore expensive clothes. And he was only partially blind, so it must be easy for him to get women interested in him with his sweet talk.

'Try me,' he challenged.

'Okay, so tell me what I am thinking now,' she said, wondering if she was doing the right thing by encouraging the conversation.

Shouldn't I just ignore him and disconnect? He, of course, cannot be a mind reader. That is impossible, because that can only be explained by magic, which does not exist. She recalled a Netflix series, *Once Upon a Time*, which had fairy-tale characters woven into a single story. Magic played a very prominent role in it.

'You are thinking if you should talk to me or not; you think a lot,' he said.

'That was a lucky guess and, actually, every stranger would think the same in this situation, where a man claims he can read minds,' she said, giving him a half-smile.

'True. Then try thinking of something I can never figure out about you,' he suggested

Her mind went back to the report she had submitted to her boss, Hardik, before leaving office.

Will Hardik appreciate my efforts or will he not be impressed? I've worked so hard on it. I have spent four precious days on it, when I could not even sleep in peace.

'You are thinking if your boss is going to like the report you gave him today. And which you took four days to complete.'

'What? That is impossible!' She was flabbergasted.

She could not believe him. No stranger could have ever made such an accurate guess, no matter the level of intelligence. The report, her boss, that the boss was male, and four days—all specifics.

'Still wondering if I can?' he asked, but this time she did not respond. If he was really a mind reader, she would not be required to say anything but only think, which she was already doing. She could control her words but not her thoughts. In fact, her thoughts were aflame. At first, she thought that it was some kind of mind game that he was playing and could really be a wise person, but the very next moment she felt scared.

What if he really can read my mind? Can he use it to discover my secrets? Perhaps try to take advantage? Should I be scared? Should I just run and get down at the next station? Or should I just stand at the door? Maybe then he will not be able to read my mind.

'Don't be scared. I am not going to take advantage of you,' he said.

Why are you telling me this? Showing off or what?

'I have not spoken to anyone in months. I was bored, so . . .'

And why have you not been speaking to anyone? What a creep . . .

'Because since the day I have recovered from my accident and lost my sight, I have been able to hear people think, and I know they hate me for it.'

Till now she had still been in two minds about whether he could really hear her thoughts, but now she believed him.

But why would people hate you?

'Because I was ruthless, like a dictator, who cared only about money and results. And now no amount of money can get me my eyesight back. I am affluent and own a billion-dollar company, and yet I have no one to share my pains with.'

Then what are you doing in this second-class compartment of a local train? Billion-dollar? Seriously? Do you think I am going to believe that? This stupid magical mind-reading stunt, and now a prince in disguise! How cheesy!

'No one knows me here, so they won't judge me or think ill of me. I feel safe here.'

Why can't you improve? You have money, the power to read minds, and here you are, crying about your poor social skills. Huh! What a story you are making up!

'I am trying, but with so much judgement already in people's minds, it is difficult. And now, with my weakness known to them, all they want to do is teach me a lesson.'

You have been hard on them and now they are doing the same thing to you. Don't you think you deserve it? Even I am judging you, even though I have known you for just a few minutes. You sound creepy to me.

Normally, she would not be so blunt in pointing out someone's flaws but she had no power over her words today, as her thoughts were open to him. She had no control over what he heard.

'I do,' he smiled. 'And maybe I don't even deserve a second chance.'

Everyone deserves a second chance. We are all human and we make mistakes. Sometimes small, sometimes big. I have made many. I was once guilty of almost cheating on my boyfriend but he was kind enough to forgive me. Yes, later we parted ways, but I understand how badly one can need forgiveness after the realization of one's mistakes. You should keep trying. Maybe one day they will forgive you. And with your mind-reading power, it will become easier for you to say the right things at the right time to people.

'You think so?' he asked. Thankfully, he did not latch on to the confession she had inadvertently made.

Not sure, because I barely know you. But then, you do look like a genuine person. Just a spoilt one, perhaps, because of all the money you have that makes you so proud.

'Then how about we have coffee and get to know each other?' he said, smiling.

All the other heads in the train turned to him. For them, he had mostly just been talking to himself, and now looked like a stalker who had caught hold of a helpless lonely girl on the train. Their eyes had a fury that he could not see but she could. Their thoughts had questions that she could not hear but he could.

'So you are asking me out on a date?' she said, to save him from the embarrassment.

He smiled and said nothing. She smiled back and wondered how impressive he would look on a date. She could no longer hide her feelings, which was disturbing but also reassuring, because she did not have to pretend or wear a mask before him. He was one man on this earth with whom she could be herself. And she would never appear any worse to him, as he was already a man who was judged by so many for being ruthless. She knew that their conversation would go a long way and that she was ready to meet him again.

On the opposite bench, the man just smiled.

9

The Genesis of Luck

Ruby Gupta

Everybody tells me I'm lucky. I have everything a woman could possibly ask for—a rich, well-educated husband, two beautiful well-behaved children and a smoothly running home. After so many years, I, too, have almost started subscribing to the belief that I am a privileged woman. But only almost.

During the early days of my marriage, I had been a giddy teenager. In the excitement of my new husband, wardrobe, jewellery, parties and picnics, I had nearly squashed a niggling voice that said, 'There's something missing.'

Of course, my children, who came soon and in quick succession, helped me channelize my thoughts and energies from my inner self. I was a doting mother and, despite having house help, loved doing everything for them myself. But once the children started school, I began to feel out of sorts. And as the kids grew and began to get alarmingly independent, the voice returned: 'You can try your best to delude yourself into thinking that you have everything, but the truth is that you yearn for something.'

The voice inside me was right—the tormenting little devil! I did crave something. I lay awake at nights fantasizing about it, and tossed and turned during my afternoon siesta aching for it. The more I tried to suppress my longing, the more it came back with renewed vigour.

Actually, it all has to do with my husband, Nishant. No, it's not what you think. He's really very nice. I think he is the most gentle, laid-back person you could ever come across. But that's just it. He is a bit too . . . I don't know . . . I can't explain it. But the thing is, I don't feel anything for him. Yes, it's true—I don't feel a thing! I mean, sure, he is very nice and all that, and I like him, but there's no spark. And certainly no love!

Having grown up on a steady diet of Mills & Boon, Barbara Cartland, Harlequin Romance and our very own Hindi films, I'd been waiting all my life to fall in love.

It never happened in school, and I had barely started college when my marriage to Nishant was 'arranged'.

To my petulant 'I want to be in love and then marry', my mother said, 'Love will come. Nishant is perfect for you in every way, and soon you will find yourself deeply in love with him. That's the way this is meant to be.'

Being the dutiful daughter that I was, I accepted my mother's argument—there was no reason not to. I liked everything about Nishant.

But now . . . now I wonder . . . Even though I like him, why don't I love him? He, in turn, seems to certainly love me and has proclaimed it often enough. So what's wrong with me? Do other women who get into picture-perfect arranged marriages also feel the same way?

Delicately, I asked my best friend, Roma, 'Do you . . . umm . . . love your husband?'

'Of course, what a stupid thing to ask.' She looked at me as if I had lost my mind.

'I mean, is it real love? True love? The love they talk about in books and movies?' I persisted.

She hesitated. 'Of course it is real love. What you are talking about only happens in stories. Real love like what I have is much better!' she said emphatically.

Going by what Roma told me, I tried to revise my thought process. Perhaps what I felt for Nishant was indeed love. I liked everything about him . . . perhaps it was not liking, it was love. Having never experienced the emotion, I had no idea what it actually felt like.

After that, I settled down into happy domesticity. But try as I might, the longing would not let up. Slowly, I began to go mad with the fierce desire to love and be loved, and it gnawed at my insides. Sometimes I caught myself staring unconsciously at other men. I felt terribly ashamed of myself. I would berate myself and try to be content with my life. Maybe I was abnormal, I thought.

This status quo would have continued had Milind not come into my life. He was the most vital symbol of manhood that I had ever seen. I can never get over my first sight of him. It was a lazy Sunday morning and I was lolling on the terrace, languidly flipping through my favourite book of poems, letting the sun dry my freshly washed tresses. Casually I looked up. And there he was, bending over his motorbike, wearing the shortest of shorts. I sucked in my breath as I looked at his strapping frame, his wide shoulders and his brawny biceps. He turned and seemed to look straight at me. My stomach lurched as I gazed at his chiselled face—all planes and angles. It was not cast in the conventionally good-looking mould. But the hypnotic eyes, crooked nose, full lips, overlong tousled hair, stubble dotting the obstinate jaw . . . all held an appeal that made him irresistible.

That evening I was filled with despair as I looked at Nishant. Try as I might, I could feel nothing for him. Nothing! There was no chemistry! I knew I could no longer continue like this. Milind had added a touch of reality to my yearnings.

After several weeks of torment, I decided that I had to do something. 'After all, you only live once!' the devilish voice inside me spoke.

Milind was the only child of our elderly new neighbours. He was probably a late-born to them, I surmised. After engineering, he had taken admission in an MBA course from one of the most prestigious universities in the country, which happened to be located in our city. I studied his daily routine and came to the conclusion that his early-morning jog was when I could get to know him. My years of yoga and exercise would come in handy now.

Soon enough, I was jogging alongside him and managed to strike up a tenuous friendship. I was delighted to find that I thoroughly enjoyed my conversations with him. He was intelligent, aware, articulate and vibrant. The hour-long jog would magically whiz past in his scintillating company. It was just so much fun! I truly came alive when I was with him. These mornings became the high point of my existence.

Truth be told, even though age-wise I was supposed to be . . . umm . . . not that young, inside I never felt not young! My body, mind and heart seemed to believe that they were just about sixteen. Actually, the Bryan Adams song, *Eighteen Till I Die*, was my anthem and I believed that it should be on my epitaph, if I ever had one. I wondered whether other women—people in general—felt this way. We grow in years but remain the same kid inside. In my head, the others were 'aunties' and 'uncles', but I was a young girl. God, too, had connived with me on this, and ensured that I looked incredibly young, which was all the more reason for me to feel like a teenager. For, whenever I looked into the mirror, the almost-child-like face that smiled back looked innocently endearing. And this is no exaggeration, I swear.

I wondered if what I was doing was wrong. But I could not help myself. I was falling for Milind and didn't want to stop. For the first time in my life I was feeling excitement and euphoria for another person. Was this what was called love?

Perhaps . . .

Whatever it was, it was exhilarating, intoxicating, and I did not want to let it go. I was becoming addicted to this giddy feeling that Milind aroused in me.

Meanwhile, I could see that Milind, too, was smitten with me. I would catch him looking at me when he thought I wasn't looking. He would drop in at my house on some pretext or the other and call up several times. He even made friends with the children . . . Both the children began to idolize him somewhat, for he seemed like a cool dude to them. Very often, when Milind was not out with his university friends, the four of us would play cricket or some game in the evenings, or just put on some music and dance. Nishant always came home late from office—and that suited me just fine. More and more, Milind preferred to hang out at our place, for his parents preferred a quiet house. Several months went by, and the happy friendship between us became deep and seemingly permanent.

One day while jogging, I twisted my ankle. The searing pain took me by surprise, and I sat down moaning in the middle of the road. Milind stopped and looked at me, worried.

'I've twisted it,' I mumbled.

'Here, lean on me. We'll rest for a while under those trees nearby,' he said gently.

As he helped me up, the pain shot up again. I sank to the road again with an involuntary 'Ouch'.

'Don't worry, I'll carry you,' he said, looking very concerned.

He lifted me into his arms. With my arms around his sinewy neck and back, I felt like a girlish Mills & Boon heroine. With lowered eyes, I gazed at the faint perspiration dotting his upper lip. I don't know whether it was the ankle or the proximity to him, but I began to feel faint. I rested my head against his shoulder. He shivered. As he was about to lower me on the dewy grass, I looked straight into his eyes, letting him look deep into my soul. He inhaled sharply and leaned into me as though about to kiss me. Then, coming to his senses, he jerked back and laid me on the grass. His breathing was fast and shallow. He lowered himself next to me, careful not to look at me.

After what seemed like an eternity, I broke the silence. 'Milind,' I began, my voice throaty.

He turned towards me.

Looking at his compelling face, I was unable to speak further. I only knew that I had these mad feelings for him. I wanted him to be mine—and reason, logic, society be damned.

He saw the emotions flit across my face.

'I'm in love with you,' he said gravely.

Hearing the words, a fierce, ecstatic joy coursed through my entire being. I felt as if the very depths of my soul had become submerged in a sea of happiness. This is what I had been yearning for, this was what made life meaningful, what would make my life complete, my mind chanted.

'I love you,' I whispered.

At these words, Milind leaned towards me and took me in his arms. Gosh! I felt aroused, content, safe, secure, satisfied, comforted and excited . . . all at once. I was home at last.

Keats's words washed over me from deep within my subconscious:

Their arms embraced, and their pinions too;
Their lips touch'd not, but had not bade adieu.

'But your husband?' Milind broke the spell.

'I have never loved him.'

Milind nodded.

'But yes, he is, of course, my husband—the father of my children.' There was no denying the cold reality.

He put a finger to my lips. 'It's okay, I understand,' he murmured, reaching down and placing a gentle kiss on my forehead.

This simple gesture made me feel cherished in a way I had never experienced before. Words were unnecessary. There seemed to be an ethereal, yet tangible bond between us that was way beyond our mortal selves.

Now my life goes on as before—peaceful and serene—except for my passion for Milind. And whenever anybody comments on my good fortune, I can truthfully agree and say, 'Yes, I really am the luckiest woman in the world.'

10

Untold Affection

Aarthika Mathialagan

Selva stared into the void as he pressed the receiver of his landline to his ear. He felt as if his heart would explode; he could feel it thumping in his mouth.

Come on, Selvadurai, talk to her . . . Say something. Anything. Just talk.

Selva was boosting himself up, and then 'click'.

Somebody picked up the phone.

'Hello?'

It was her. He struggled to breathe. He tried to talk. It was as if his tongue was stuck. He slammed the receiver down, and slowly walked to the terrace of his house and climbed up the water tank. He lay on the Pattamadai mat, staring at the moon. Selva had lost count of how many times he had tried to talk to her—in school, over the phone and so many other ways. But he just couldn't. He had even tried to prevent himself from falling for her and maintained distance from her, but all his efforts had turned out to be in vain. The more he tried to stay away from her, the more he yearned to see her and be near her. Her absence only sharpened his feelings for her. He tried to sleep. But he knew he wouldn't be able to.

The next morning, even before the rooster's call, Selva was awake. All the women in his neighbourhood had started with their morning chores. As usual, Selva, on his terrace, was waiting for her to come out, so he could look at her as she slowly made the dots and gracefully joined them for her *kolam**. Then he would leave for school early and wait for her to come.

He loved waiting, for her.

Selva had understood that the pain in waiting really had some pleasure in it. Then he saw her. With the tinkling sound of her anklets filling the silent dawn, she came to their *vaasal* (threshold) and started placing the rice-flour dots for the kolam. Selva's day was incomplete without seeing her design the kolam. It had been like this for three years, since Selvadurai fell in love with her. Bhavani.

It was in Class VIII that Selvadurai first saw Bhavani. It was not love at first sight. There was no attraction, no fast heartbeats or butterflies in the stomach. Conversations were easy, no awkward silences and no waiting. Bhavani was just his classmate then. It was in Class IX that he started seeing her differently. She was not the same girl any more for him. Something about her had changed. He couldn't place it exactly, but things were definitely not the same between

---

* Kolam is an auspicious design drawn on the floor with rice flour, which also acts as food for ants and birds.

them. He slowly started to look at her during classes, missed her when she was absent, and smiled when she laughed. He thought he just liked her, that he was merely attracted to her. Then slowly this attraction and infatuation turned to love—sheer one-sided love.

Like every morning, Bhavani had washed her hair, plaited some of it and left the rest down. Selva loved the way she tucked some of her lustrous locks behind her ear. She always had this small smile on the corner of her lips. Maybe she knew he was watching her. At least Selva thought she did.

'Bhavaniiii!' he heard her mother call her. She hurriedly joined the dots and ran inside. This was the moment that Selva thought made all the waiting worth it. Every morning, Bhavani threw a small glance at Selva as she drew the kolam; it was not even for a full second, but his stomach flipped and it was as if his whole world depended on that one microsecond glance. One look from her was all it took to make Selva go crazy. In these three years, all the songs were about her, everything reminded him of her, all he did was to impress her, to get a second glance from her. He was so much in love.

And then, 'Selvaa . . . come down now or you'll get it good from me.'

It was Selva's mother. He ran down to get ready for school.

~

Moorthi, Ramesh, Jawahar and Selva were 'the inseparables' of Class XI. All the three knew about Selva's affection for Bhavani. At first, when they knew, they teased him mercilessly and called out his name when they saw her, even pushing him towards her in the corridors. But as days passed, their teasing changed into cheering and they started encouraging him to talk to her. But never once did Selva have the guts to. Not that he never tried, but just looking at her made him sweat and go tongue-tied.

That morning, the three boys were eagerly waiting for Selva. Jawahar raised his eyebrows enquiringly as Selva arrived. Selva answered them with a shake of his head. All three of them sighed. Selva sat with them and again thousands of ideas were given, along with hundreds of criticisms, and while they were talking, Bhavani came into class. She usually sat on the first bench and Selva on the fourth. The teacher was taking their attendance and it was now that Selva watched her. He just sat there and looked at her. He felt ecstatic just looking at her. He loved looking at her. But in these three years, not once had Bhavani turned around to look at him. All Selva could see was the back of her head, but still his eyes never moved. He hoped to see at least some part of her face.

The teacher continued calling out the names when suddenly, Bhavani turned and looked at him. All this time he had yearned for that look and now that it had happened, he didn't know how to react. His stomach flipped. His legs shook. The space between the collar of his shirt and his hairline started burning. He looked at his friends to see if they had seen what had just happened. But nobody seemed to have seen her looking at him. He wondered if he had started hallucinating.

Why did she look at me? Did she really look at me? Am I imagining it?

It was as if he was going to get a panic attack. There was this ticklish, yet stinging feeling in the area between his stomach and his chest. On the other hand, he was floating. That whole day all Selva could think about was that moment when Bhavani had turned to look at him.

'Maybe she's giving you a sign, da,' Ramesh told him while almost choking on his medu vadas.

'But what if it's just a coincidence?' said Moorthi.

'I don't think it's a coincidence. If it was, why would she look at Selva? She could have looked at me.' Jawahar, as usual, was feeding Selva optimistic thoughts. Selva was tuning his father's new Pagaria radio to a new station. It was playing his recent favourite from the newly released film, *Roja*.

Thendral Ennai Theendinaal Selai Theendum Njaabagam;
Chinna Pookkal Paarkkaiyil Deham Paartha Njaabagam;
Velli Odai Pesinaal Sonna Vaarthai Njaabagam.

(The touch of the breeze reminds me of your sari,
Small beautiful flowers remind me of your body,
The silver stream speech reminds me your words.)

The song was too much for him. He felt his heart wrenching. He loved her so much that it had started to hurt. These were feelings nobody would understand. He also knew that this feeling would be his and his alone, and that it could not be shared. But that was the nature of unrequited love—giving it your all and expecting nothing in return. What if she never returned his love? What if he was unable to stop loving her? These questions frightened him. But he couldn't stop thinking about her, and he knew his feelings were true.

He decided to do it. That night, he decided to tell her how he felt about her.

He dialled her number and waited. It rang a little longer than usual. Just when he was about to hang up, someone picked up. It was her. But there was no usual 'hello'. Just breathing, long and deep breathing. Both of them stood in their houses with their receivers pressed to their ears and listening to each other breathing. Neither of them spoke. As Selva tried to match the rhythm of his breathing to Bhavani's, she spoke. 'Selva . . . meet me tomorrow in the chemistry lab after class.' And disconnected the call.

Selva just stood there. She had just spoken to him and it still hadn't sunk in.

She knew? For how long? How did she know it was me?

He would have to wait until tomorrow for answers. He went to the terrace and tried to sleep. However, he knew it was in vain. All he could think about now was what she was going to tell him tomorrow. He closed his eyes and recalled how his name sounded on her lips, the way she pronounced it . . . and slowly drifted off to sleep.

The next day in school was painfully long. Every minute took hours to pass. He felt as if a big boulder had been placed on his chest. As time passed, it became difficult for him to breathe. The final bell rang and it was as if an adrenaline shot had been administered to his body.

The boys as usual fed him ideas of how to talk to her, and sent him off.

Selvadurai started walking towards the chemistry lab. He was going to meet the girl he had loved for three years. In no time he was there. He stood at the door. He couldn't enter the lab. Bhavani was already inside, looking at the pipettes and the burettes like she was looking at them for the first time. Selva just stood at the door, looking at her. She saw him and smiled. Selvadurai felt his heart jump to his throat. He stepped inside and slowly walked to her. Both of them were silent for some time. The awkward silence was overwhelming.

Finally, Bhavani turned to him and asked, 'Selva, do you like me?'

Selva didn't need to think to respond. 'I love you,' he said.

He couldn't believe he had finally confessed his feelings to her. She didn't say a word. Her face was empty of emotion. She walked to a window and leaned against it. Selva, not knowing whether to go near her, just kept standing there.

'You want to stand near me?' asked Bhavani. Selva walked to her. He had been dreaming of this moment for years and now that it was happening, Selva just stood there, not knowing what to say.

'Do you . . . do . . . I . . . uh . . .' Selva couldn't get the words out.

Bhavani smiled. 'I like you too, Selva. Don't know since when, but I like you too.'

She didn't say anything more. And he didn't want to ask anything more. Both of them kept staring out of the window in silence. They had a lot of time to talk, but now that they were together they both needed this silence with each other.

She had waited for his call every night, learnt new kolams to impress him every morning, stolen looks at him when he played kabaddi with his friends, and even had songs that reminded her of him. But she could tell Selvadurai this any time. They didn't know if they would get this time together in silence again. They cherished it. Both of them had big smiles on their faces. They didn't know what future had in store for them, or if they even had a future together. They were only in school. They had their whole lives ahead of them and a lot to learn. But, at that moment, Selva and Bhavani were in love. And their love took its own time to develop. Both of them had gone through the pain of having feelings they could not share with anyone else, and both of them knew how it felt to know the other person was reciprocating their feelings. Selva gulped every time he saw her and she remained silent the whole time. But they had taken the first step to togetherness, from unrequited love.

11

I'm No Good Human

Mohammad Afroz

Listen, girl . . .

Don't fall for me, I'm no good human.

I'll be soft at the beginning, caring, loving. I'll stand by you when you or your family need me—of course to gain trust, because everyone who is good at heart wants other people to do good and make them believe that good exists. I'll play this game of make-believe. I'll hide my insecurities, try and act like a perfect human, give you freedom, make you feel as if you're the most important person in my life.

I'll not only bring you chocolates and roses, but remind you that your period is around the corner and make it my priority to check if you have your sanitary pads, as well as chocolate bars to keep you company during your mood swings. Just to act like I respect the goddess within you. I'll sacrifice my dreams, needs, time and sexual desires so

I'm not marked as a person who wants to satisfy my lust. That's my main motto, though—I'll keep this for the perfect moment when you will be the one 'asking for it'. When I'll not be able to control my testosterone any more, I'll make weird demands and emotionally drain you to fulfil those. But midway I'll realize that snuggling was more important, so, with tears in my eyes, I'll ask for forgiveness. Crocodile tears, mind you. It's an act.

I'll write you sweet letters, emotional ones, alarming ones. I'll write sonnets, poems, even a poetry book, but don't give in—it's all because I want to label myself as a perfect match. The kind people crave for, the ones they write about in undying incomplete love stories. I'll even tell you beautiful lies about how your smile makes me float, how awestruck I am and how your eyes elevate me to the heavens. I'll plead to God to create words and verses to write in your praise. I will want to woo you in every possible way. That's why I'll wait for you—in the sun, in the rain, or when you want to see me to find courage, power and strength, so that you know I am always there.

But don't bother—it's just an act. Remember, I'm no good human. Remember this.

I'll remember birthdays—yours, your sister's, your little brother's and your mother's. Remember the day we met, hugged, kissed, went on our first date, first movie, first family function, my sister's wedding and your sister's book release? I'll even write speeches for your mother, because I'll be good with words. I'll bring them gifts, chocolates, happiness, support and also treat them as my kith and kin, and tell you repeatedly how they are not yours or mine, but ours, and that we will keep them happy and hopeful forever.

I'll even mend that broken pen and that toy gun, and if I'm not able to do it, I'll buy new ones to replace them. I'll get your phone with the bad microphone repaired; I'll say that it's because I can't hear your voice properly, but the real reason will be to pretend that I care about your little things too. I'll also try to mend the trust that you've lost in men, because all I want to do is make sure that I am one of the good ones. Long live feminists and feminism!

I'll always sound interested in you, your memories of your younger self. I'll ask for photographs, to see how you looked in your childhood, and when you won't notice, I'll sneak one and keep it to myself—keep it in my wallet or inside a book that I read too often. I'll ask for favours, and if events come up and you're not able to make them, I'll criticize you and say things that'll hurt you, make you feel like you don't give me enough importance. You'll be disappointed in me, in my behaviour, and then I'll act like I'm genuinely sorry for saying those things and that I got angry because that event mattered to me. When you'll ignore me, I'll shed a few tears. Men do not cry, but I do, just to make sure you don't think of me as that not-so-strong man who hurt others.

Because it's young love, I'll try and remain calm when you are having your mood swings. I'll confirm if you still have chocolates; you'll nod, but the irritation will reflect in your eyes, so I will let you pass sarcastic remarks. But listen, I will just be acting like a wise and understanding man.

I am no good human—I'm the worst kind!

I'll take you to meet my mother; I'll try and get you comfortable with her so that you two can get along in future, just to tell you that I don't date for fun, that I'm serious. But all that will be a myth; remember, I'm no good human. I'll make some promises, fulfil them just so you fulfil yours too. It's a trade-off, you see—a promise for a promise.

I'll get the fuel pump of your car repaired while you party with your friends on your farewell—because, hey, we drove this car, and it broke down in the middle of the road and I had to push it all by myself on that hot, sunny afternoon, even though I felt faint on my way to the garage. But I'll make sure that it's repaired while you party. And hey! Guess what? Even though I had been vomiting the previous day, for I was sick, just to show you that I'm strong and responsible, I'll pretend I'm okay. But in reality, I'll be in need of your warm touch and want to cling to you—but remember, I'm no good human. It's to see that you don't hang around with your other friends—other male friends. Not to mention it's been months since we met, as I was busy looking for a good job so I can one day ask your mother for your hand. Besides, I will find one, and it will be my first leave, so that I can be with you. It'll be a planned sick leave. But don't bother, I'll be there to keep an eye on you and watch you while you admire that beautiful white sari. But I'm just here to stop you from hanging out with other guys. With my first stipend, I'll buy clothes for my mother and yours, and a chocolate for you—your favourite—with the leftover change. Chocolates will give you the idea that

I remembered you too. I'll start buying you more gifts, roses and more chocolates, and when you ask me as why I'm wasting money, I'll say they were cheap flowers or that I got the gift on offer or that Big Bazaar was giving out free chocolates with a pack of my favourite Oreos.

I'll motivate you to start looking for a job too, so that you can help with the expenses of your family. It'll help your single mother a lot. And when you find a shitty call-centre job, I'll remind you of your dreams and ask you to go after them and not this—but since you'll not be taking my advice any more and feel that I'm trying to control you, I'll put up an act at that time, okay? I'll understand.

I'll cry a little that you'll be leaving for a few days and how I'll not be able to breathe the air around you—but remember, I'm no good human, and this is because I don't want you to get along with the other people at the new place you are going to. Someone will bring you to your senses, and you won't go, and I'll hear someone else tell you that it was because I was controlling you. You should listen to them. They'll be right.

With Christmas and New Year around the corner, I'll want to be the first person to wish you, because my happiness comes from you, and the magic within you is the symphony that I want to drift off to. But remember that I'm no good human—it's all because of the Christmas cake you bake so well, and the New Year party. I have no one else but you, so I have to pretend it's because I love you, because other people, friends, family and colleagues understand that you're more important to me and that is why I was not there when they needed me—I was with you. So now I don't get invites for New Year parties, but I have to be happy, so I have to pretend I'm happy being with you.

Your uncle's family will visit your place—it's their mother's home too. We'll not be able to have proper conversations as you'll be too busy to take my calls. You'll not reply to my texts, probably because they'll be around. And I'll say that I understand and will give you time with your family. And I'll be busy too. My exams will be underway—important for me, for us! I'll bag a government job if I get through. I'll study hard, because I want to secure our future. But remember, I'm no good human—it's because I want to show you that I'm a man worthy of any girl. And a government job does that. Money in the bank, honey! With money in the bank, you can be a bad human being. Love is only a small, diminishing culture; money is the new sexy.

When your uncle visits you, he will find you a suitable groom, and you will have to compromise, because it will bring shame to your family to marry for love. I'll only marry for love. The new guy will be rich, good-looking and well settled, with a great job—and he will be a good human being. I'll plead with you to fight for us, you'll say you can't, you'll ask me to talk to your mother. I will. I'll explain to her how much you mean to me, how much I have loved you. I'll say that I know that I don't have a settled life as of now, and I'll ask her to talk to your uncle. She'll promise me she will. I'll go for days without food and sleep; I will go to the mosque more often to plead in front of the Almighty, but you, on the other hand, will be interested in the other guy. We'll talk less frequently over the phone; you'll get irritated with me, you'll ignore my texts while being online every time, because you'll be talking to the other guy—the one you want to marry. Because now you know I'm no good human.

The exam I was talking about will be on a Sunday; you'll also have the same exam. We'll go to the exam centre together, maybe for the last time. I'll hug you while I'll leave for mine and plant a small kiss on your forehead. In three hours the exam will be over and we'll be returning home. You'll promise to get home and call, but you won't, because now you know I'm no good human.

You'll not take my calls; you'll ignore my texts even more. I'll plead with you to talk to me one last time and that I'll never disturb you again. You will. I'll tell you about my incompetence, about how all I ever wanted was to hold you and sleep, rest my heavy eyes on your bosoms, maybe sleep the most beautiful sleep of my life. I'll say this just to tell you how much I've loved you. You'll tell me that I should sleep; this will be the last time I'll be hearing your voice over the phone. But guess what? I will record this call. I'll hear your voice every night over and over again while I imagine myself sleeping in your arms. But remember, I'm no good human—this was all for my mission, my carnal mission. And, well, if we sleep together, there's bound to be sex, right?

I missed the chance.

It's good for you, though, but I'll remember that call. Things will not be over yet, but you'll make me feel as if they are by not replying to my texts—and exactly at

1.11 a.m., you'll send a text: 'Everything's finished now. Someone told the other guy about us, about you loving me, and told him that I was no good human.' I'll wish it was you who had told him. You'll say, 'We are just friends.' Were we only friends?

And you will start to blame me, and feel it's okay to switch rides, because life is a roller coaster and everyone should try a different ride. Your mother will call the next day, asking me to talk to your maybe future fiancé and husband, because she thinks I'm a good guy. But you know the truth. I'm no good human. But since your mother thinks I'm a good human, I will do it. Because I'm still acting to be a good human being. I'll call your fiancé, tell him the truth—that we are just friends—and end the call with a question: 'What do you do?' Answer: 'I work in an IT company. I am well settled, have a flat in Pune and a good bank balance.' He'll not tell me this—I'll just understand. He is a good human being.

Without you it'll be tough. I'll tell my mother everything. She'll cry. She'll know I loved you too much to live without you. She'll cry, and that'll be the act of a bad human being, because I made my mother cry. I'm no good human.

I'll be distraught watching you go. I'll hope a miracle will happen. I will hope. But your good human being is now someone else. All I can do is look at our old photos, relive our old memories, write sad poems and sonnets, post statuses with us together and pictures of us holding hands— and guess what, miraculously, your fiancé will see them! I was fighting myself to find purpose, happiness, a reason to live. I think I'll adopt a baby girl, give her your name—maybe I'll be a good human being to her.

And when I'll be fighting everything, your mother will call. She will start the call with 'You're no good human', and everything will go crazy, and I'll hear your voice, 'Ask him if he was the one who did this.' I will shiver, I will quiver, and feel a benumbing pain inside. My legs will feel paralysed, my head will spin and heart shatter into a million pieces. I guess everyone will have figured out that I'm no good human.

My mother will be furious. She'll call your mother and they'll talk. My mother will say, 'They loved each other—at least my son did.' Yours will say, 'Your son destroyed my daughter's life. He's no good human.' My mother will then say with a smile on her face, 'I know.'

So I'm no good human—everyone knows this. I can't be trusted and, at every instance, I'll make it clear.

But this cliché of love—'I'll do everything for love'—is so beautiful.

Don't fall for me. I'm no good human.

But remember that though I may not be a good human, I'll love you as one.

For sure.

12

Pure Love

Praneetha Gutta

Today, Ria came to me with a notebook when I went down to have breakfast.

'Ananya, Mom told me to give this to you,' she said, and ran out of the house to play with her friends. Though at first I was surprised to see my personal diary after so many years, I started to flip through its pages and reminisce. After settling down comfortably on the couch, I opened it. It was my diary, which I'd started writing when I was eighteen. That was the time I got to know that I was already married to my uncle's son, Siddarth.

I was told that when I was two and Siddarth five, my mother was hospitalized as she had a brain tumour and got to know she didn't have much time left. Since I'd already lost my father in a road accident when I was a six-month-old baby, she wanted my life to be secured. She asked for her brother's son's hand for me and he readily agreed, as it was her last wish. So, at that time, according to Hindu rituals, we were married. From then on, my aunt and uncle have taken good care of me, as if I am their own child. They have never differentiated between me, Siddarth and his elder sister Gayathri. All three of us played together and spent a lot of time together. Whenever I remember those days, a smile comes to my lips. Uncle did not speak to me about this marriage until I'd completed my secondary education. That was when Siddarth was working very hard to get into international cricket, and most of the time was away from home. I, too, left Ahmedabad and went to Kolkata for my graduation. There I stayed in a hostel, and this diary became my closest companion.

Coming out of my thoughts, I shifted my concentration to the words I'd written in the pages.

07.09.2008

Hi diary, I am Ananya. Now I am eighteen and I stay in a hostel in Kolkata. I want to introduce you to the most important person in my life.

Siddarth: my world.

You have been very special to me since my childhood. I think maybe because we spent most of our childhood together, sharing so many sweet memories. You were always there with me whenever I needed a shoulder to lean on or whenever I wanted to share my happiness or worries with someone. Of course, anyone who has witnessed or experienced your love and care can never hate you. And I would never wish to go away from you. Okay, you might be wondering why this dumbhead is becoming so emotional now, right? It's because today is your birthday, and this is the first time in so many years that you are celebrating it without me. Anyway, many, many happy returns of the day, Siddarth! We will meet soon, when your tour is over. I will be waiting.

Reading this page, tears rolled down my cheeks. Again, I went back to my memories.

~

Siddarth visited me whenever he came to Kolkata and we had a lot of fun roaming the city, trying out its different cuisines. The way he always took time out of his busy schedule for me increased my respect for him. I didn't realize when I started falling for him. It was in 2010 that Uncle and I decided to tell him about our marriage. I remember I was so happy that I could be with him forever. But I wanted to tell him this news once he was settled properly, so that he wouldn't have any distraction. That's why we had to wait. But then I didn't know that destiny was playing a game with us. That very day, when we decided to tell him, I got a call from him. He sounded excited.

'Hey, Ananya, you know what? I am so happy I finally proposed to her!'

I was shocked, but composing myself, I asked, 'Who? Who is this girl, Siddarth?'

'You know her too, Anu. She was your classmate in school . . . Do you remember Sakshi?'

'Oh, Sakshi . . . Of course . . . She was the one with the curly hair, right?' I tried to sound normal.

'Yes, the same beauty with brains. When I went to Mumbai for a tournament a few months back, I met her in the hotel where the team was staying. She was . . .'

He was telling me about Sakshi, but nothing was registering. I was lost in my world of disbelief and confusion. Should I be happy or sad? Finally, I found my voice.

'Congratulations, Siddarth! I am so happy for you. I will talk to Aunty and Uncle about her today. Come home soon. Bye!' Saying this, I disconnected the call. And for the first time in all these years, I felt a void in my life.

Though my brain was telling me to be selfish and not help him, my heart wouldn't do it, so immediately after composing myself, I went to my uncle to speak about it. I knew it wouldn't be easy to convince him, but I knew I had to do this for Siddarth's happiness. He should not suffer for something that had happened even without his knowledge.

'Uncle, he loves her,' I said after explaining what had happened. 'Most importantly, he will be happy with her. Please try to understand. Don't ruin the life of two souls for one promise you had made to my mother. Even she wouldn't be happy if her children were unhappy.'

'Then what about you? Don't you want him in your life?' asked Gayathri, as she was the only one who knew that I loved Siddarth.

'I will be happier to just see him smile, even if it is with someone else. I won't think twice before giving him what he wants. If I tell him about my love or our marriage, he will surely leave her and come to me. Then I will just be his wife and nothing else. I don't want to be that. I want to be in his heart and be the reason for that smile whenever he remembers me,' I told her with a heavy heart.

They were against it in the beginning, but later, seeing my stubbornness, they agreed. As our marriage had not been registered, I felt there was no need for Siddarth to know about it.

~

I turned the pages of my diary where I had pasted many pictures of Siddarth. The last picture I remembered sticking was his marriage photo. But I was surprised to find the remaining pages of my diary filled by someone else. It was all written beautifully. It was all about Siddarth and his special moments, both professionally and personally. I was so happy to read all of it that I decided to speak to Sakshi about it. So I went looking for her. I found her sitting in the lawn playing with the dogs and watching Ria play with her friends. I sat down beside her.

'Hey, Sakshi. In the morning Ria gave me my diary and told me that you had asked her to give it to me. I was surprised to find all this,' I said, showing her the photographs that had not been pasted by me.

'Why? You didn't like them?' Sakshi asked with a smile.

'No, no . . . They are awesome! I . . . ' I couldn't continue, as realization dawned.

'Relax, I was the one who continued to write in your diary.'

I looked at her with so many emotions roiling inside me, tears welling up in my eyes. She held my hand.

'Ananya, I found it near your bed in your room after you left us eight years ago. Maybe because you left in a hurry, it got misplaced. I found it and read it. I know I shouldn't have—it is your personal diary. But that was when I got this idea to continue writing in it and thought would gift it to you when you returned. So I am not regretting or apologizing for it,' said Sakshi. I smiled at her, letting her know that I didn't mind.

There, we sat in silence for a while. We were both lost in our own thoughts.

I recalled how I'd left for the US after their wedding to complete my master's and then settled there. I never wanted to return as I was afraid that in some weak moment or the other, I would end up making Siddarth feel guilty for something he didn't even know anything about. But a message from Sakshi had brought me back to India last week.

A few days back I got a message from her saying that my uncle's condition was serious and that he wanted to see me. I came to know it was a prank to get me back to India. Though I was angry with them initially, I couldn't stay angry for too long after seeing Siddarth's cute little daughter, Ria.

I was shaken out of my thoughts by Siddarth's voice, 'Hey, come in. Let's have lunch. I am feeling hungry. By the way, what is this you are holding in your hand?' He took the notebook from me.

Before I could stop him, he was turning the pages. 'Wow, it is more like my album. Who did this?'

I looked at Sakshi in panic. She calmly smiled and said, 'We both did it—only for you, Siddarth.'

Siddarth exclaimed 'Great! This is amazing! By the way, girls, where is my birthday gift?'

'Your gift is standing right in front of you,' Sakshi said, holding me by my shoulders.

With a smile, Siddarth took my hands in his. 'You know what, Anu? When you were leaving for your master's, I thought no one would tolerate this dumbhead for more than a year. I thought . . . wished . . . they would throw you out of the country and you would come back in a year or two. I never imagined in my wildest dreams that you would take eight long years to make it back. How could you have stayed away from us for so long? You don't know how much I've missed you all these years. Sakshi had to tell a lie to get you here, because you are always making excuses to not come to India.' Hearing his trembling voice, I hugged him and let my tears flow. After composing myself I broke away, saying, 'Now no more emotional talk.'

Taking my diary from him, I called out to his daughter, 'Okay, now let's get in. Ria, baby, come on! It's lunchtime.'

We celebrated Siddarth's birthday and, at night, I sat down in my favourite place beside the window and started writing my diary again.

07.09.2018

Today after a long time, I enjoyed a lot—that, too, with my favourite person on his birthday. I have met many of your teammates and had a fun time, Siddarth. I can't forget this day anytime soon. Many, many happy returns of the day. You are getting old, my dumbo!

With a sigh I closed my diary and lay down on the bed, lost in my thoughts for the final time that day.

After I left India, I searched for my diary in my bag but couldn't find it. I had never expected to see it again, but look at life's irony—now I have again started writing in it and will continue to till I have strength in my hands. Thank god I hadn't written anything about our marriage in the diary. Now I am more than happy to see Siddarth like this and don't want anything else in my life.

You will always have a special place in my heart, Siddarth. It is eternal, and nothing will bring it down to the level of obsession or possessiveness. Maybe this is what is called 'pure love'.

Love you, Siddarth, forever and ever . . .

This was my last thought before I drifted off to sleep.

13

Beyond Right and Wrong

Supreet Kaur

Somewhere beyond right and wrong, there is a garden. I will meet you there.

—Rumi

It was 11 p.m. on a chilly Delhi night. My hands and feet were cold, but one of my cheeks was warm, red, with blood rushing through it. I could hear my ears ringing as a tear rolled down my other cheek, as if trying to sympathize with what had just happened.

My dad was standing there, his hand still in the air, ashamed of having slapped his twenty-five-year-old daughter, hiding that shame in the form of anger.

'Get out of my house right now!' With this, he held me by the arm, opened the door and started dragging me out.

'But Dad, listen . . .' I said through a choked throat.

I looked at my mom with welled-up eyes for help.

'You were the good one . . . We were so proud of you. What happened?' She struggled to get the words out amid uncontrollable crying.

As I struggled to stay indoors, my dad let my arm go, suddenly regretting what he was doing with the daughter he loved so much. He did not utter a word this time, but went back into his room, slamming the door hard, leaving me and my misery behind. Mom, too, walked away.

Sitting in the doorway, my heartbeat and thoughts raced.

I had been the most adored daughter of the family, but I'd made just one mistake to change it all. I had fallen in love.

~

It had all started with an office trip to Bengaluru a few years back. Scared but excited at this opportunity, I had managed to convince my overprotective parents—and I was finally out of my protected environment.

~

Nervous about my first day in office in a new city among new people, I dressed up in all black to give a sleek first impression. I had called one of my colleagues the night before, informing him of my visit and asking him to help me with access formalities. He and I had been working together for a year. I knew him by his voice on official calls and the fact that he was the most helpful person in the team.

Waiting in the lift lobby, I was looking out of the window of the eighth floor, taking in the views of the city, lost in my own thoughts, when I heard his voice call my name. I turned.

He was 5'9, dressed casually for a Monday in relaxed-fit jeans, an off-white half-sleeve T-shirt showing off his toned arms and a sleeveless black hoodie on top.

'Welcome to Bangalore.' He smiled, extending his hand towards me. Staring into his dark brown eyes, I took his hand in mine. His hands were rough and hard, matching his toned arms. My small, soft hands felt protected in that firm, warm handshake. Little did I know in that moment that these hands would be there to stay.

The days in office flew by with stringent deadlines and tonnes of work, but it was the late evenings and weekends that made me feel lonely. So I started staying back late at the office rather than returning to the guest house. I was tired of eating by myself every night.

While leaving office around 8 p.m. one day, I saw him working. In dire need of human company, I went to him.

'Do you want to grab dinner?' I asked.

'Ah, okay,' he said, but there was hesitation in his voice.

We went to a nearby dhaba.

'I am missing Punjabi food so much!' I said, sounding desperate.

He smiled at me and then pointed to the waiter.

'*Bhaiya*, one dal makhani and one shahi paneer,' he said.

In that moment, he was my knight in shining armour. It was my first satisfying meal in the city.

The way to a Punjabi's heart is through the stomach. That night was the start of a new friendship. We started spending more time together. More dinners, weekend movies, harmless flirting, blushing, finding excuses to touch each other's hands . . .

The freshness of early infatuation was a magical feeling.

~

Magic doesn't last long, as I soon discovered. It gives you a temporary high but ultimately brings you back to the real world. My magical period of one month was over. It was time to head back home.

'I don't think we'll ever meet again . . .' I said, holding his hands in the office parking.

'We will,' he replied, looking deep into my eyes. Then he kick-started his bike and left.

I just stood there, looking at him disappear, with a strange hollow feeling in the pit of my stomach, a lot like Simran in *Dilwale Dulhania Le Jayenge* standing at London's Kings Cross station after she bids adieu to Raj, not knowing what a mess she had stepped into! Coming out of my trance, I got into my cab and left for the airport.

~

Back home, I got busy with work, family and friends, but Bengaluru was always in my thoughts and conversations. I felt some part of me had been left behind in the city. Maybe it was him? Was I really missing him? I have had many crushes in the past, but none of those feelings have lasted so long. I was craving to talk to him. But what should I suddenly talk about after so many days? I picked up my phone and forwarded a joke as a conversation starter. He responded with an emoji. There I was—skin in the game!

As time passed, the jokes changed to good-morning and good-night messages, the chats changed to calls. We started sharing all the details of our day; slowly he earned his place as my 3 a.m. friend and gained top position on my speed dial.

~

'I am coming to Delhi tomorrow for a day,' he messaged me one day. I was nervous. I would be meeting him for the first time after Bengaluru. This last year we had come so much closer. But I had also heard of people who had talked a lot over the phone and through messages but had trouble connecting when they finally met. *What if that happened to us?*

With hundreds of questions in my head and butterflies in my stomach, I went to the airport to pick him up. My hands were sweaty, my throat dry. While continuously adjusting my hair and my new dress, my eyes were intently scanning everyone coming out of the airport gate.

There he was, this time more maturely dressed in a green-and-blue check shirt, blue jeans and an army-style haircut. As he came closer, I extended by hand to say hello. Instead, he leaned in and hugged me.

With his chest against mine, I could smell his intoxicating perfume. I felt an invisible spark run through my body. It was a new feeling, different from everything I had felt before. *Love?*

This meeting was the big leap that took our friendship to a new level. We started meeting more often, planning occasional intercity trips.

Soon we were officially in what the world calls a long-distance relationship. From 'more than friends' we became a couple.

~

The distance sometimes grew due to our separate international office trips and demanding IT jobs. When travelling abroad, we started putting in more effort into activities that we could do together irrespective of time zones; staying awake late to talk, adjusting our mealtimes to eat together, and enjoying the charm of late-night video calls.

But no matter how advanced the technology, it still couldn't replace the warmth of his hug, the taste of his lips, the protectiveness of his hands. Phone calls were no longer enough—I started craving for more. I started missing him all the time. On some days, this feeling was so strong that I wished I could step into the damn laptop and hug him.

After looking for a job change for a few months, he finally found one in Delhi. This marked a huge step forward in our relationship. We met more often, went on dates more often; our understanding increased, insecurities reduced, and we found comfort and solace in each other.

~

Nobody went down on one knee or screamed with excitement. There was no drama—but there was a proposal! And it happened this way:

'Our kids will never misbehave this much,' I said to him while pointing to a wailing kid at the mall one day.

'All kids are like that—even ours will be the same,' he replied nonchalantly.

What?! What the hell had we both just said? Were we already envisioning our kids in the future? Such old-school lovers we were! We both looked at each other as these words came out of our mouths.

His gaze held mine. It had a question, I could sense it.

'Yes,' I said, and the deal was sealed.

~

I am Sikh, he is a Brahmin from northern India. It is not just a cultural shift—these are two different religions. Our gods, our places of worship, our family beliefs are miles apart.

Only an Indian kid will understand the insurmountable odds in breaking to a conservative family the news that she is in love with someone from a different religion.

The whole night I kept rehearsing versions of this conversation in my head for the next day's chat with my parents. Little did I know that that day, my world would change forever!

That night, with one cheek smarting from my father's slap and my mom crying in front of my eyes, marked the end of that conversation.

The slap was still fresh in my mind—the first one of my adult life!

The next morning, after the family drama, I mustered up the courage to call him.

'I think we should call it off,' I said, crying. I was traumatized from the events of the night before; I had brought out the worst in my parents.

He resisted, begged, pursued me to give it another try and to stay positive. He kept assuring me that he would make things right. But I had made up my mind to sacrifice love for my family. Maybe we were never meant to be.

'Maybe I am not strong enough to fight the world. I love you, but I love them too,' I said. And with this last conversation, I severed all contact with him.

~

This self-initiated break-up started taking a toll on my health. I missed his hands in mine, the comfort of his voice, which made me believe the world was still a good place. I was sure he was in the same pain. I couldn't focus on work. I stopped being happy.

Months passed. The leaves on the trees started turning yellow. Watching them fall made me cry and reminded me that those leaves would forever be away from their trees—just like I was from him. It was my birthday in two days and I knew it was going to be the worst birthday of my life. I just wished that Earth would revolve a little faster so I could jump directly to the next day, saving myself the pain of having to go through this day without him.

I wanted to be as distracted as I could on my birthday. An empty mind generates negativity. I went to office and started working half-heartedly at my desk, forcing myself to concentrate. The phone rang—it was him. I declined. He called again. I again declined. After his third call, I decided to pick up as an exception, politely accept his birthday wishes and get it over with.

'Hey,' I said.

'Look to your left, idiot!' he shouted on the phone.

There he was, outside my office bay, crazily waving at me.

My eyes welled up. I was motionless. Tears started rolling down my cheeks.

'Come outside,' he mouthed and waved again. I stood up and rushed towards him as if in a trance.

'Why the hell are you here?' I shouted after reaching him.

'Shut up!' he said softly and hugged me tightly.

With one touch of his warm body against mine, I started crying loudly. How much I had missed this comforting touch, this reassuring voice!

In that very instance I knew that I could not stay away from him any more. It had been a stupid idea in the first place. We talked a lot, shared so much that was buried

inside of us all this while. We were back to our old selves—
we were back to being 'us'.

We realized that what we had was too precious to let
go. We had to continue nurturing it, protecting it from
those who didn't understand it.

~

Being the kind of daughter who shared everything with her
mom, I wanted to run back to her again and tell her how
much I still loved him. I wanted to tell her I could not be
without him. However, every time I tried talking about it,
the reaction was the same as it had been the first time that I
broke the news to them. I could no longer take it. I could
no longer relive the worst day of my life. I stopped sharing.
I stopped trying to tell her. My dad stopped discussing this
topic at home, assuming his daughter was as obedient as he
expected her to be and that I had been able to switch off all
emotion inside me.

On the other hand, he and I continued to meet and
cheer each other up. I was back to being happy again. My
morale in office was back. I was no longer crying. The
environment back home was also coming back to normal as
I was no longer discussing him.

~

This is our tenth year together.

We have found our middle ground—not together but
not apart.

From a mutual break-up to planning a milestone trip to mark our anniversary, we have grown up.

With fulfilment in our hearts and excitement in our eyes, we have completed our road trip early this year.

Driving through the empty roads one late evening, with Arijit Singh playing in the background, and another failed attempt at GPS with poor network, we are literally on the road to nowhere. We have no idea where it is taking us.

But despite this uncertainty, we are at peace. This moment is symbolic in our lives.

Not all love stories move towards closure in the same way. For some, the journey itself is the destination.

~

We are both doing great in our professional and personal lives, fully committed to each other—in sickness and in health, for better or for worse, for richer or for poorer. The only exception is we are not living together; our relationship doesn't have a legal name and there is no document we have signed.

Our families have still not come to terms with it. Things have been left unsaid, undiscussed and have been assumed to have died. We are tired of fighting with them. At some level, we understand their concerns, but we can't fully agree with what they want either.

We have found our happiness beyond the clichés of society. Life is all about being happy; however you define it or quantify it, everyone measures it differently.

We have found our happy place. This is our garden, beyond right and wrong.

14

Once Upon a Love . . .

Suranya Sengupta

It was in the early Seventies that I lost my father. At eighteen, barely an adult, I had to quit my studies quite reluctantly and join the first job I could find to sustain my widowed mother and little brother. The working hours at the factory were quite long and I didn't mind them, only for the smile of relief I received from my mother when I handed over my hard-earned money to her. I had it all planned—how to progress with work and make sure my brother's education was not hampered—until life happened unexpectedly one day.

Every day I passed by her lane—a short cut on my way back home. I could reach my house a few odd minutes before time. In the fairly empty dark alley, her veranda provided the only light on my way. She would sit there, on the first floor veranda on a swing, her long hair braided on either side. She would swing gently, reading a book or humming a tune to herself. I would often see her gazing up at the star-studded sky. It was pretty late for anyone to be on the streets—my job was new and at odd hours. The city slept by the time I managed to get out of the factory. The light from her veranda would fall on the concrete lane below, helping me see in the dark. I would look up on an impulse, and some days our eyes would meet briefly before I would walk away. I was always in a hurry. My mother would be awake. I needed to get home. At times, it felt as though her eyes would light up every time I looked up at the veranda hoping to find her there.

Had it become a habit seeing her there, or did she actually wait for me every day?

One evening, a storm shook the city. It poured heavily and the streets were waterlogged. I struggled to find my way through the alley, cursing myself for not bringing an umbrella. Summer thunderstorms were unpredictable. As I neared the illuminated veranda, looking up at it almost out of habit, I saw her holding something in her hand. I neared her house, and suddenly there was a plastic bag thrown down at me. Jolted by this unexpected gesture, I ducked, yet it landed on my head. She giggled. I looked up with a smile and she ran inside, conscious of the fact that I'd heard her laugh at me. Inside the plastic bag was a blue umbrella. With little yellow flowers printed on it. I stared at the empty swing before putting the umbrella over my head. It protected me from the rain drops for the rest of the way. I smiled in gratitude. My mother was surprised to see me dripping wet, yet with an umbrella over my head. She asked who it belonged to. I didn't know why I lied. I said it was a colleague's.

Was it difficult to say it was hers because a stranger had helped me? Or because she was no longer a stranger?

The next day I carefully wrapped it in the same plastic bag. With a note saying 'thank you' in my native language. I was not sure if she would understand it, but my knowledge of languages was limited. She had been my saviour on a disastrous night. She needed to be thanked.

That night when I hurried home I stopped below her veranda. I looked around to check the empty alley. Her eyes opened a little wide, watching me stop. She got up from her swing and came up to the railing, leaning over just a little, watching me anxiously. I was a pretty good thrower in my gully-cricket team—a skill that once got me the newspaperboy's job in the neighbourhood in my early teens to support my school education. That day my skill helped me land the umbrella safely back on to her veranda. To my surprise, she waved at me. I obliged.

Days turned into months without any words exchanged. Sometimes it was a wave of a hand, sometimes just smiles; most of the times we just gave each other acknowledging stares before I walked past her veranda and she went inside. Something in me knew she would wait, no matter how late I got; something told me she knew that I knew. How strange are these silences that speak more than a thousand words ever could? I could never have believed the poets if not for her.

One of the days, however, she was not on the swing. Instead, she was standing on the edge, leaning over the veranda railing and staring at my end of the lane. I frowned. I noticed that her skirt didn't match the blouse she wore with it. And that she had kajal in her eyes. It looked like she had dressed up. It was unusual for her. Her braids were always neatly oiled. Her cheeks shone in natural radiance and she had a tiny mole on her chin. I was a little embarrassed as she blushed when she saw me stare. In a trance, as though captivated by her deep dark brown eyes, I waved. She waved back with a smile lighting up her eyes. Then she was gone. I wanted to talk to her that day. She probably wanted to hear me as well. But not a word came out of my mouth. It was as though I was stripped of the ability to speak. I had never expected such feelings, never even dreamt that a well-spoken person like me would not know what to say to someone. I had also rehearsed in my mind several times during work what I wanted to tell her—things about me, who I am, about my family and, most importantly, where I stayed. My slum house was nothing compared to the mansion she lived in. I sighed and walked away.

For the next few days I tried in vain to bring words to my mouth. It felt like forever. Every day I would work hard and wait for the evening. Every evening I would take the short cut home. Once in a while, when I stopped to wave, a toffee, a chocolate or a packet of biscuit would land my way. I carefully saved the wrappers after eating the goodies.

I had bought some ribbons and chocolates with the money I'd saved from my tiffin and given those in return. She had smiled the next day, flaunting on her braids the ribbons I had given her. Sometimes I was happy I couldn't talk to her. What if she judged me after knowing who

I was? What if the education or the status I never had was important to her? Could I afford to get hurt and end the dream that was keeping me going? I often lay awake at night and wondered about the possibilities. I was no match for a girl like her—well brought up, educated and beautiful. But could I ever feel this way again? Did I even want to feel this way with another person?

One day her veranda was empty. The lights were off. I shuddered. Was she unwell? Had her parents found out? A sudden fear of losing her gripped me. A strange urge to knock on their door overtook me. But I restrained myself. What would I say? Who was I? The question was left unanswered.

Two days later, she was on the veranda again. My eyes lit up in happiness. She smiled, knowing I had been worried. I waved my hand in a questioning gesture: *Where were you?*

She touched her forehead: *Fever.*

Worry swept across my face. But just then, someone called her inside. That was the first time I got to know her name. I walked away with a smile of relief. She was fine. Everything was fine.

The next day a piece of paper landed softly on my head. I looked up as she hurried back inside and shut the door to her room. Frowning, I picked up the piece of paper. There was a scribbling in pencil that couldn't be deciphered in the shadows of the alley. That night, while my mother slept, I read her first letter to me. Her handwriting was childlike. The pencil seemed to have been sharpened more than once in the letter. She had asked my name, where I stayed, why I was late every night. I stayed awake till dawn, heart thumping, writing my first letter to her.

The letters continued for almost three years. The pencil scribbling turned to scented papers and ink. I improved my vocabulary just to impress her, and started reading books again. She recommended quite a few. We discussed poetry in our letters.

One evening, along with a letter, her teary eyes haunted me: *Take me away with you. My marriage has been fixed.*

Her unsteady scribble didn't let me sleep that night. I twisted and turned in my bed. Was I brave enough to hold on to love? I didn't know the answer. She had unknowingly put so much faith in me. Her face, her smile, her giggle, her tears, her fearful eyes haunted me. I got up early at dawn. I found myself outside her veranda in broad daylight, sleepless. It was like the heart was fearless now. It wasn't afraid to hold on. I threw a stone at her veranda and waited. She ran out. Did she know it was me? Of course she did. The twinkle in her eyes met my smile. Her eyes were questioning. I nodded. I saw her cheeks wet with tear drops. I wanted to wipe them off. I wanted to hug her and never let go. I wanted to hear her talk, listen to her sing, know what she smelt like, how soft her touch felt. I wanted to know everything then and there.

Almost like a flash of lightning, things happened. Her sister caught us exchanging letters. Her father walked out and threatened me. People gathered, gasping and whispering comments on my character and my upbringing. Her brothers held my collar and pushed me down to the ground. My eyes didn't leave hers as her mother held her arm tightly. She wept, she begged and she said she loved me. For a moment my heart stopped, before it started beating faster. Amid the noise, her voice was all that mattered, her tears were all I could see. The crowd was looking at us like we were criminals. Her parents ordered me to leave. I shoved past her family; I gave her my hand. I asked her to take it. I told her I promised nothing but love. She said she didn't need anything more than that. Her father slapped me. Her brothers beat me up. The neighbours hurled abuses at me and threatened to hand me over to the police. I returned home bruised in heart and mind. They locked her up.

For three days I tried to catch a glimpse of her in vain. On the fourth day I was a warrior. I knocked on her door, surprising her father. She ran out and I gave her my hand again. This time she let go of her mother and ran to me. Her soft, warm hands touched mine. For the first time. And for the first time I felt like I was complete, a man with a purpose. She made me that. Her eyes spoke a thousand emotions. She hugged me, and I promised to never let go. People gasped. Her family threw out her belongings. They reminded her that their door was shut to her forever and that she was dead to them.

My mother first looked shocked and disgusted when I brought her home, after learning about what I had done. The neighbours said a love like that happened in stories. Real life was different and harsh. The girl was making a big mistake, and that I had my eyes only on her money. My mother put up with all the taunts hurled at us and soon became our biggest supporter.

Thankfully, those were better days. Although love and a marriage of choice was judged and often criticized beyond a point, the families later accepted. There was no honour killing. Our parents still loved their children more than society or religion. Love was rare—and respected. Choices made were honoured and promises kept. No one could stop lovers who decided to be together. No one approved of them either. But we had our own way with the world. We painted our own world away from norms. We were romantic warriors. Our cousins and friends worshipped our actions while their parents winced at it. Did we care? Once I knew my house had become a home for her, I gave her all the love I could. I was complete. We were complete.

~

Today, my son introduced his choice to us. Her religion was different. Her family threatened to kill him when she confessed of their relationship to them. He looked unsure of what they were doing, their commitment and love, if their earnings would be enough to sustain them and whether they could live through their differences and make a home in harmony. His questions troubled me. His mother looked worriedly at him, then at me, as though she'd read my thoughts—like always. I looked at my son's troubled eyes as a thousand insecurities showed up in them. He was not ready to commit to her, on a life threat. He was practical, unlike us. He knew he had choices. I accompanied him to file an FIR against the girl's parents and hope for the best. And somewhere between the legal formalities of threat and protection, I found that today love had lost a battle with society—the love that his parents had lived was simple, blameless and boundless . . .

It was a feeling of pure, unadulterated love, without the complexities of society's imposed boundaries that made us doubt our feelings for each other, and the commitment it needed—to choose each other against all odds, every single day, for the rest of our lives.

15

Yesterday Once More

Sarbani Ray

As the figure approached her, smiling, treading on the red-brick walkway of the garden, Ananya experienced a sense of déjà vu. The chant of the morning hymn from the prayer hall, together with the red sky, a prelude to the rising sun, resurrected the past in perfect precision. The years lost their numbers as she went forward to meet him, with the light steps of thirty years back, on the other side of life. She was about to call out the familiar name, when, out of nowhere, Urna appeared.

'Oh, you are here on time, for a change. That's really great! Mom, this is Ahan, my friend and the class topper. I told you about him.'

'Yes, of course.' Ananya stopped, suddenly feeling heavy on her feet, and slightly drained from the moment's agitation. Still, she kept looking steadily at the face of the young man in front of her.

Ahan, an otherwise smart person, smiled nervously, uncertain of the intense gaze fixed on him. Ananya could sense his discomfort, but couldn't take her eyes off the face. The young man was a spitting image of Rohit!

Was it real, or her imagination, fuelled by the surroundings of their youth?

'That's an exaggeration, Aunty. Urna herself has done so well, grabbing an excellent package in campus recruitment!' Ahan responded to Urna's outburst, and the friendly exchange that followed helped Ananya regain her composure.

Urna had always been an independent girl. Studying in her mother's alma mater was her own choice. Ananya never interfered with Urna's decisions, unless absolutely required. Fourteen years back, when she and Ranjan had decided to part ways, Urna, aged only six then, had decisively expressed her willingness to stay with her mother. Ranjan, too relieved, never looked back, severing all ties with them. He always blamed Ananya's success in her career for his own failures.

Surprisingly, Urna never seemed to care much for a father figure. From a very early age, she was a strong woman, quite capable of standing on her own. Sometimes Ananya sensed a role reversal between them. Her corporate job took most of her time, in the city or on tour. Urna, meanwhile, managed her studies and home all by herself. Ananya wished she had been that strong at Urna's age!

As Urna and Ahan talked about various programmes that had been arranged during the course of ceremony, she sat there in the familiar setting of her youth, counting the changes that had appeared over the years. She had come here on Urna's admission day but hadn't got a chance to look around, as the stay was too short.

The main garden, with the prayer hall at the centre, still remained the same, so did the old banyan tree. The vice chancellor's house, which stood adjacent to the north gate, had been converted into a library now. She wondered what had happened to the old library building, where she'd met Rohit for the first time. It was really odd that two shy and silent people like them had fallen so desperately in love soon after their first meeting!

There was not much left of that girl in this strong and confident corporate manager of today. She was still soft-spoken and reticent, but now the silence had a strength beneath it that had been absent earlier.

Urna never showed any of her traits at her age—always bursting with energy, talking, debating and making friends. The courage, which in Ananya's case had been acquired while traversing the rough paths of life for years, was an inborn quality for Urna.

Being a natural leader always, Urna led her mother and Ahan towards the famous dhaba, outside the main gate, for breakfast.

On reaching the dhaba, Ananya enquired about Sahuji, the owner from their time. It was his eldest son who ran the place now, and Sahuji, he said, had gone back to his village.

Sitting on the wooden bench outside in the sun and gorging on tasty aloo parathas, the three of them chatted about various issues.

Ahan had overcome his earlier awkwardness and Ananya, too, had started enjoying their youthful conversation, leaving aside the reminiscences of her past.

On their way back to the guest house, Urna reminded her, 'Mom, you are coming to our class dinner tonight. Earlier, it was for us students only, but now, on popular demand, families have also been included.' Ahan echoed the plea.

Ananya gave a sigh—this was probably the time to meet her nemesis. Perhaps destiny had their meeting planned this way, for, after watching Ahan closely, she was certain he was Rohit's son.

Not only his face but his build was also similar. The difference lay in their mannerisms. Ahan had a cheerful countenance, whereas Rohit always bore a serious, almost gloomy face.

But then Rohit had not been lucky enough to have the carefree days of youth Ahan enjoyed. He had had to worry about the situation at home, especially after his father's sudden demise, which had left the family with very little means. His ailing mother and sister had been waiting for Rohit to get a job soon and improve the condition at home.

Still, in those moments of intimacy, he would smile silently at her, and the love in his eyes would make his features soft, malleable. How Ananya longed to wipe out the creases of worry from his face and bring love poems back to his pen!

On reaching the guest house, Ahan left to make arrangements for the night. Alone with Urna, Ananya decided to have a straight talk with her daughter.

'Ahan is a nice boy, I don't remember you mentioning him before. What took you so long to introduce me to him?'

'Why, mom? You have hardly met any of my friends from college as you . . .' Urna stopped mid-sentence and looked thoughtfully at her mother. The very next moment, she burst out laughing,

'Mom, stop it! Don't get ideas. Ahan is only a good friend, like many others. At present, we are all just shaping our careers ahead! No time for anything else. How could you even think of it?'

Her daughter's candid confession eased her mind a bit. Then she thought about why it should matter to her at all! Throughout the day, Ananya continued to argue with herself, framing logic and counter-logic, and finally concluded that her daughter's choice of partner was none of her business!

In the evening, she started to dress for the party. Urna, seeing the beige sari she had chosen, objected rather firmly, 'Mom, you are not going to wear this dull colour, specially for this evening. You must wear your blue silk. You look gorgeous in blue.'

These were exactly Rohit's words. He would always insist on her wearing blue.

Anu, you should see yourself through my eyes. Blue suits you like no other colour does. I see a piece of sky meeting the ground when you walk in blue.

Ananya hesitated a little, but then decided to go with her daughter's wishes. It didn't matter, really, after all these years. Rohit would be at the party with Ahan's mother, a proud parent of the class topper. Both the charm of the colour blue and of its wearer must have long faded in those eyes.

As she entered the hall, her heartbeat grew louder. Urna was greeted by cheers from all sides—from her friends and teachers. Ahan was on stage, playing the guitar with a band. Ananya looked around for Rohit but could not find anyone like him among those present. Had he changed beyond recognition or had they not arrived?

Some of Urna's friends came to greet her and introduced her to their parents. The band was playing soft, pleasing tunes. Ananya started to enjoy the party, which was well organized, with very subtle and aesthetic arrangements. There were some alumni present among teachers and parents. A woman from her junior class, who remembered her well, showered compliments on her.

'You are still so pretty, Di! Not many changes other than a little extra weight, which, by the way, suits your personality.'

Time passed happily, reminiscing of old times.

The band then started to play the timeless anthem of graduation, a favourite of their times—*Papa Kehte Hain.* This was Ahan, singing loudly with his guitar.

Ananya looked everywhere but could not see anyone resembling Ahan's 'papa' anywhere. His friends surrounded the stage, clapping and cheering. Urna was leading the noisy crowd from the front. The elders stood a little towards the back, encouraging and smiling. After all, you are young only once!

As dinner was announced, Urna guided her mother to a table and brought soup for the two of them. They had just started when Ahan came to them, with a lady and a gentleman.

'Aunty, my Ma and Baba. *Maayi*, you have met Urna already; this is her mother, Ananya Aunty.'

Ananya had noticed this couple earlier, standing quietly near the stage and listening to the music. Ahan's father nodded at her respectfully and his mother held Ananya's hand intimately.

Disappointed or relieved?

She was not sure of her feeling—a bit of both, perhaps. They sat together with food on their plates. Ahan and Urna did not give anyone much chance to speak. While recovering from the state of dismay, Ananya could not help but glance at Ahan's face from time to time for a more detailed look. His likeness to Rohit was uncanny. Nature had played a trick on her!

That night, Ananya dreamt of the Urni river.

She had often taken a walk along the riverside with Rohit. He would talk about his dreams, their future together and read poems to her. She'd named her daughter Urna, as the child's laughter had reminded her of the river and the joyful memories associated with it.

In her dream that night, she saw the silver line of Urni and the sparkling white sand of the riverbed on a moonlit night.

Rohit, drenched in moonlight, recited Nazim Hikmet to her: 'You'll live, my dear. My memory will vanish like black smoke in the wind.'

She awoke very early the next morning. Urna was still sleeping. Quietly, Ananya slipped out, past the garden, and started walking towards the river.

The pristine beauty of the river and the surrounding jungle remained intact, untouched by the hand of time. A little out of breath from the long walk, she sat down on the ground. Time, too, went past her like sand, as she sat there, immersed in the stream of memories.

A soft touch of hand brought her back to the present. Ahan's mother was standing by her side.

'Ananya, I am Rohit's sister, Ruhana . . . Ruhi, remember my name?'

The calm in the voice touched Ananya. She stood up and looked straight at her for a few seconds, trying to grasp the meaning of those words.

So Ahan was Rohit's nephew. Now that explained the resemblance!

Ruhana looked at her hard, as if trying to read her mind.

'You guessed right before. Ahan is Rohit's son.'

Confused, Ananya stared back at Rohit's sister. Yes, she was his sister all right; the similarities were distinct.

'Ahan's mother died at childbirth. Rohit was very upset. He blamed himself for not caring for her enough—for not being able to forget you, ever. He decided not to marry again and took up a job abroad. I kept young Ahan with me.'

Trying hard to hold back her emotions, Ananya said grievingly, 'I am sorry. It was my fault that I couldn't gather enough courage to go against my father at that time. But Rohit was not ready for marriage either, as he had family responsibilities. I, too, have suffered a lot. I have failed in my relationship.'

Suddenly the years melted away, and past and present merged together. The vision of a girl with a dupatta drenched in tears, sitting on the edge of her narrow bed as her father roared outside, came alive in her mind.

How dare she want to marry someone from a lower caste with no proper earning? It will take him years to stand on his own feet and rise to any kind of socially acceptable position. All love will go down the drain when they struggle to make ends meet. This is outrageous! I can't let my only daughter throw her life away because of a street beggar!

Ananya now felt a surge of pain for the younger Ananya going through the emotional turmoil, praying silently for help.

Oh, she was so young and stupid, perhaps, to believe in those empty threats!

Tell her that if she leaves home to marry that boy, she will not see me alive again. I will prefer to die than bring shame to my forefathers because of her. The status we have gained in society over generations will be dust in one day. If she wants to build her life on her father's grave, let it be so.

Ruhana's voice sounded distant. 'Don't be so hard on yourself. Perhaps it was fated to happen. And see how destiny has brought you two on the same road once again. On one of my visits to Ahan, I met Urna and discovered that she was your daughter. She is such a loveable girl, and we bonded really well. I heard of your divorce from her.' She added tenderly, 'Rohit loved to talk about you. I feel I have known you all my life. I always considered you a sister.'

Ananya eyed her gratefully. Rohit had never said much about Ruhi, except that her marriage had been a priority for him. It would have been nice to have had a caring and compassionate human being like Ruhana for a sister.

'I told Urna and Ahan about you two. Kids of today are more mature than us. They are the ones who planned this meeting for us during the graduation ceremony. Urna kept it a secret from you as she wasn't sure how you would react to the idea.'

Ananya let her tears flow. Ruhana held her tight.

A group of four was seen walking towards them.

'Here they are now. Rohit landed yesterday evening and took the night train to get here for Ahan's graduation. He, too, was kept in the dark until now. He is as bewildered as you are about this whole situation. You two have been silently suffering for too long now. We all feel that life should offer you a second chance.' Then, with a sharp intake of breath, she said, 'Ananya, don't disappoint my brother this time.'

From afar, Ananya could see Urna clinging to someone's arm, happily waving at her. She couldn't catch the voices over the sound of the river. Then the group halted and one of them started to move towards her.

She stood there, staring at the approaching figure, a repeat act from the previous morning, leading to a similar upheaval inside her, but of a very different sort this time. Tears got washed away in smiles. The sun, the river, the breeze and the trees all cheered in unison at this happy college reunion.

16

Platform 9 . . . and 3/4?

Sashwati Ghosh

Florence, Italy

1750 hours

Amid the flurry of people, the monotonous pre-recorded voice announcing the arrival and departure of trains, her eyes scanned the crowd in a heightened sense of excitement and anxiety.

Where was he?

Indira was standing in the underground passage of the train station, in front of the staircase that led up to Platform 9. All around her, people were frantically rushing into the passage and darting up the stairs to the platforms where their trains were about to leave. It was the middle of December, and chilly winter winds drafted through the station.

Indira pulled her rainbow-coloured scarf tighter around her neck and tightened the belt on her cherry-red coat. Amid the dull grey and black tones of her surroundings, Indira was like the first bloom of spring. She was tall, slim and undeniably attractive, with long, wavy hair that framed her heart-shaped face and wide-set dark eyes that now glanced anxiously at the fluorescent board displaying the scheduled trains.

Her heart began to pound erratically as she saw that the train that would bring him from his office in the outskirts of the city to Florence had arrived five minutes early.

He was here.

Any second now she would see his 6-foot 2 frame cutting through the crowd and making his way to her on Platform 9. From there, they would board the 6.04 train home, to the humble town of Pistoia. And they would have, for almost one uninterrupted hour, conversations that would touch the strangest of topics—and, in turn, her heart.

This had been their routine for a couple of weeks now, travelling to and from Florence together—she to the university and he to work. She was a budding architect, and though she loved her classes and the time she spent with her friends, her daily commute was what she looked forward to the most.

She often thought about how quickly she and Prithvi had become friends. It had barely been a month since they'd been introduced by common friends. She thought about Prithvi more often than she cared to admit. Prithvi was like a breath of fresh air in Indira's life. He never mulled over things like Indira did, always acted on instinct and never hesitated to say what was on his mind. She loved that he was such a free spirit.

1800 hours

The train was due to leave in four minutes. And Prithvi was nowhere to be seen. Waves of disappointment washed over her as she contemplated the idea of a journey without him. Suddenly, from her left, a soft voice, eerily close to her ear, whispered 'Ciao, cara!', and she nearly jumped out of her skin. She turned to see Prithvi laughing uncontrollably at her expression. She was still catching her breath as she gave him a playful punch and allowed him to gather her into his arms for a tight hug.

'I'm sorry!' he said, the twinkle in his eyes betraying him.

'Yeah, you look really sorry!' Indira teased. 'I thought you couldn't find me! And, as always, your phone's out of charge!'

'Indu, I could spot you from a mile away in that scarf,' Prithvi laughed, playfully giving her scarf a tug.

'So I like to wear some colour! I'm making up for the people around me,' Indira told him matter-of-factly, raising an eyebrow at Prithvi's all-black outfit.

He looked especially handsome that day. She had found herself attracted to him of late, but today, with his long black coat buttoned all the way up over his jeans and his black scarf knotted casually around his neck, she was left quite breathless. Not to mention that mop of floppy black hair she had an inexplicable weakness for.

'Hahaha! Touché. Ready to run?'

'Let's go!'

They bolted up the stairs to Platform 9 to find the train pulling in. Prithvi pulled Indira's arm instinctively, causing her to step back behind the yellow line as they waited for the train to come to a stop. She smiled to herself—he had no idea how these small gestures made her feel, and it was all she could do to keep it from becoming apparent.

It was a Friday evening, and people were returning to their hometowns after a long week's work. Even so, the train was unusually full and there were no empty seats left. They stood in the passage between two coaches, as other passengers continued to hop onboard. Prithvi put an arm around her shoulders as the passage filled up completely.

Okay, that's a first. Indira's heart beginning to race. *Stay calm, stay calm.*

As the train began to pull out of the station and pick up speed, Prithvi's grip on her shoulders tightened to keep her from losing balance. After a few minutes, Indira rested her head lightly against his shoulder and was surprised at how natural it felt. At this proximity, she could inhale his unique smell, which was a heady combination of musk tinged with a lingering trace of what seemed like sandalwood. The overall effect made her transiently giddy. She lifted her head from his shoulder, trying to regain her composure. At this, Indira felt Prithvi's grip on her shoulder slacken ever so slightly, with his eyes now intently fixed on her profile, wondering what had caused the sudden shift.

1830 hours

The train had covered almost half of its one-hour-long journey. In a few moments, they would pull into Prato. The people in the passageway looked weary now. The train came to a halt and people began to disembark. Prithvi suddenly pulled on her hand.

'What are you doing?!' Indira exclaimed.

'Just trust me! Let's do this. You won't regret it!' Prithvi told her, jumping off the train. Indira still stood inside, looking at him incredulously.

'You're not actually going to make me do this!'

'Come onnn . . . be spontaneous!'

Spontaneity was NOT her strong suit. Indira prided herself in leading a structured life and taking well-balanced, premeditated decisions. Prithvi was casually dismantling all her notions of how she believed life should be. Indira took a few deep breaths.

Okay, relax. This isn't such a big deal. There are trains that can take you back home every hour. Maybe it'll even be fun to explore a new town. And you'll be alone with Prithvi in a new town.

Prithvi hopped back into the train. 'Are we doing this?' he asked, looking down at her, locks of his dark hair falling into his eyes.

God, those brown eyes . . . Indira felt the last few vestiges of self-restraint slip away.

'Let's do it!' she finally said.

Prithvi flashed her a smile as they got off the train. They looked at each other and laughed as the train trundled out of the station, leaving them behind.

1840 hours

Prato wasn't as sleepy a town as Pistoia, though it came close. Exiting the station, they saw the town slowly becoming quiet, lights dimming as people shut shop and headed home. No matter how small the town, *aperitivo* was one thing that Italians took seriously. It was their version of happy hour, and if you purchased one drink, you could eat any amount of finger food that came with it.

Indira and Prithvi were in high spirits as they made their way towards the town square, an element that was woven into the architectural language of all Italian cities. The square was bustling with people, violinists and street musicians playing beautiful melodies, setting the tone for the evening. A small but quaint church framed one side of the square and a string of cafés overlooked it on the opposite side.

Making their way to one of these cafés, they ordered their drinks (a local concoction of gin and berries) and sat outside, at one of the many tables that dotted the cobblestone pavement. Overhead, strings of small golden bulbs cast a glow on their faces as the sun set behind the church. A server arrived, bearing a tray of mouth-watering dishes, starting from appetizers to dessert, all bite-sized portions so one could sample everything.

Indira's eyes lit up as she picked up a slice of pear and a cube of Brie cheese, and put them in her mouth. Prithvi smiled looking at her expression; she had her eyes closed— the exotic combination of cheese and fruit had sent her into a momentary trance.

'That good, hmm?' he asked, twirling his fork in a small bowl of creamy carbonara spaghetti.

'Better! Never tasted anything like this in India!'

'Do you miss home? India, I mean,' Prithvi asked her.

'Sometimes, but not much. I love the freedom I have here—doing things that I wouldn't be able to at home. I love how I can just take a train and be in a different city tomorrow without worrying about what Ma will say; how I'm cooking my own meals and that they're turning out even better than I thought; how I can just step out of my house, take a book to the park outside and read for hours, no questions asked; and . . . I'm rambling, aren't I?'

Indira blushed as she looked at Prithvi, who hadn't interrupted her even once.

'This is the best kind of rambling. Go on!' he urged, thinking how lovely she looked when her eyes shone as she spoke of the things she loved.

The minutes rolled into hours as Indira and Prithvi talked about everything under the sun, conversation flowing as easily as the wine the server kept pouring for them.

2030 hours

'Maybe we should head home now?' Indira asked, looking up at the ominous thunderclouds, her practical side kicking in.

'Live a little, Indu . . .' Prithvi said softly, standing up and extending his hand, gesturing towards the square, where several people had started to dance to the street musicians' rendition of *Tarantella*, a classic Italian folk tune.

As she took his hand and let him lead her to the central square, Indira shook off the last of her inhibitions. She couldn't find any more reason to resist the feeling that they were right where they should be. Indira and Prithvi fell into step beside the seasoned local dancers as the cheerful song picked up tempo.

Time seemed to slow down for them and, to Indira, it felt like they had been dancing for an eternity when the song finally ended with a grand flourish and everyone began to clap and laugh.

'Bravo!'

The crowd applauded the musicians as they picked up their instruments again and prepared for their next piece.

The violinists filled the square with the lilting strains of a slow love song. From the crowd, couples paired off and began to sway to the music. Indira and Prithvi looked at the couples around them and then sheepishly at each other.

'I don't know how . . .' Indira said.

'Neither do I!' said Prithvi. 'That's what makes it fun.'

Prithvi gently placed her hands around his neck and his own on her waist. Soon, they were swaying effortlessly to the enchanting melody.

'I thought you didn't know how to dance!' Indira gasped, as Prithvi gave her a twirl and pulled her close to him again.

'I don't. You're bringing it out in me,' Prithvi whispered into her hair.

2130 hours

'That was a really good time. It's not something I normally do!' Indira said, her cheeks flushed. They had run to the station. Prithvi looked at her and smiled; she looked quite ethereal in the gathering darkness, with the light from the sole lamp reflecting off her eyes.

As they climbed up to the platform, it began to drizzle, gusts of wind blowing towards them.

'Thanks for today,' Indira said, stepping towards Prithvi, emboldened by a rush of adrenaline.

'Come here,' Prithvi said, wrapping his arms around her with a sudden urgency. As he held her, Indira felt his head resting on hers. The train thundered into the platform and Prithvi pulled her closer to him as it began to rain more heavily.

Indira wanted to freeze that moment in time and wondered if Prithvi felt the same.

2200 hours

Indira and Prithvi got off the train and walked through the station.

'Prithvi! There you are! You're late!' Elisa, Prithvi's French girlfriend, waved at them from one end of the station.

Indira wondered if she had imagined Prithvi sigh.

'See you on Monday?' Prithvi asked Indira.

'See you Monday.'

She watched Prithvi walk over to Elisa. Elisa looped her arm through Prithvi's as they walked out of the station.

Indira realized that she hadn't checked her phone throughout the evening. She unlocked it now and felt her heart plummet.

10 missed calls from 'Aakash <3'. Indira felt as though the last couple of hours had been something out of a dream, and now someone had rudely awakened her and jolted her back to reality.

0000 hours

Later that night, Indira couldn't sleep. She knew that her life had changed irrevocably that evening, that something had changed between her and Prithvi. A barrage of conflicting thoughts flooded her mind. She couldn't help feeling a tinge of guilt at what had transpired between them and yet, she wondered whether her story with Prithvi would ever take off from Platform 9.

'Platform 9 and 3/4. Almost, but not quite,' Indira thought out loud, sighing wistfully at the *Harry Potter* reference as she closed her eyes and finally drifted off to sleep, the Italian love song playing in the background.

17

Flare

Mariam Rashid

In the City of Nawabs, in the last hour of the night, moonshine was glorifying the golden Arabic verses carved on the wall of the mosque.

وَقَالَ رَبُّكُمُ ادْعُوْنِ ىٓ اَسْتَجِبْ لَكُمْ

Moid looked at the verse and tried to interpret its meaning. It perhaps meant 'Call upon me and I will answer', but he was not sure. In his dilemma, he walked into the masjid and prayed beside a man who was in prostration, whose heart was somewhere else like most of the people around him. He prayed for the Almighty to reveal to him the real meaning of love. After his prayers, he stepped out to leave, when unexpectedly the imam of the masjid approached the young man.

'Would you care for a cup of tea?'

This sudden invitation caught him by surprise, but he accepted, and joined the imam in his small room on the first floor.

'Are you new here? I haven't seen you around earlier,' the imam asked.

'I lived here when I was a child. Then I left for the US for further studies. Then . . .' He couldn't finish his sentence.

'Are you the one writing the book on Sheesh Mahal?' he asked, his voice serene.

The young man became wary.

'So you have called me to tell me how haraam it is to write about whores?' he asked.

The old man smiled. 'No, I have called you to tell you a story. The story of a girl who was born in Sheesh Mahal.'

A puzzled expression crossed Moid's face, since he'd never seen maulanas mention brothels, especially in masjids.

'Lover?' Moid asked.

'Love.'

'Who was she?'

'Will you mention her in your book? I will only tell you if you promise to write her story.'

Moid nodded. The girl had his curiosity piqued.

When the imam got his assurance, his eyes became wet, as if he were waiting for this moment. In a broken voice, he started narrating his tale. Her tale.

'Behind the stars that hold the light, behind the mirrors that reflect the light, she was hidden in darkness. Darkness from which only light could be seen. She was the only young woman in Sheesh Mahal whose body had never been touched, whose soul had never been corrupted. Other women in Sheesh Mahal kept themselves dressed, ornamented and perfumed for any rendezvous they may have, but Mehr-un-Nisa used to wear dull colours, her messy hair tied up and hands dirty with splotches of blue ink. She smelt like an old book of fairy tales.

'The girl with deep eyes, curly hair and golden skin was never meant to be born out of wedlock in a brothel, but she was. No girl born in a bordello is meant to wear chastity and dignity with confidence, but her mother was a rebel. She taught her daughter Arabic and Urdu. But she never allowed her to go out in front of any man for her own safety. And Mehr never did . . . Except for one man, nobody had seen her.'

The imam looked at Moid, who was listening intently. 'Perhaps this peculiar expression crossed over your face because you think I'm judging the women living in brothels. But you are wrong. I'm simply narrating the events as they are.'

He continued.

'I first saw her when darkness was melting into dawn, probably at this very same hour. Under the deep-blue sky, below the crescent moon burning golden, she stood at the window, staring at the fading stars. I was going to the masjid, unaware of her fragrance. Something seemed to draw my gaze up and my eyes fell upon her. My heart skipped a beat. I stopped for a while and smiled when I spotted black ink on her face radiating the same shine as her hair. But suddenly a beautiful woman with blue eyes dragged her inside and closed the window. It was then that

I realized this was Sheesh Mahal. I was smiling at a woman standing at a window of Sheesh Mahal. But it didn't matter to me . . . It never did.

'This happened when I was sixteen. After that day, I used to find her standing at the same window every day. Sometimes she would look up at the sky, perhaps counting the stars or talking to the One who had created them, and sometimes she would smile at those fireflies playing in the courtyard. And I would look up at her as I walked towards the masjid.

'This hide-and-seek between us continued for three years. Every time I looked at her, she looked more beautiful than the previous time. Earlier, I used to ask myself why the longing of Qais for Laila never stopped, even though Laila was a Moor, even though she was married to another person and had left him. But then I started to understand as my heart slowly got pulled towards the girl at the window. But I never dared to linger for more than a few minutes. We never talked to each other. But I knew why she would stand up there; she knew I was not merely walking by to offer *tahajjud*. We know what our hearts want but we also know that's impossible.'

'Why?'

'Why? That's what I ask myself every day. Perhaps because she used to live in a brothel and I was raised in a masjid. Huh! You know every heart coming to the masjid is not pure and every heart beating in a brothel is not filthy . . .'

'Then what happened?'

'One day she sent me a letter through Husna, confessing her love for me . . .'

'Husna?'

'Husna was her maiden and a very dear friend of hers. She was the one with beautiful blues eyes who had dragged her inside the first night our eyes met. She was one of the most elegant ladies I had ever seen.'

'Continue . . .'

'I told my father I wanted to marry a girl. He was happy to hear that I had someone in mind. He excitedly asked me her name and address, and I told him. As soon as those words left my lips, the colour drained from his face. He has never been the same with me since. On that day I witnessed love transforming into hatred. I assure you it wasn't a pleasant sight. I tried to explain to him that I wasn't doing anything wrong, but he didn't think so . . .'

'What he did do?'

'He locked me up in a room—tortured me and threatened me for days. But I didn't give up. I believed my love could melt his heart—but I was wrong. He rebuked me in every possible manner. He chanted that I was a sinner. According to him, it was a sin to marry a girl raised in Sheesh Mahal. According to this world, love has always been a heinous crime. Yet I wasn't suffering because of his rebukes—the real torture was not being able to look at her for so many days. That torment and helplessness reminded me of Qais's bewilderment and I understood one more mystery of this world.

'You know, one day, cousins of Qais mocked Laila in front of him saying she was dark. And you know what he said?'

Moid shook his head.

'He replied in verses comparing Laila's beauty to musk, which is also black but rare and expensive. I did the same, but differently. But for lovers like us, it is an even greater sin to stop someone from loving, or to accuse somebody of kufr—blasphemy. According to me, marrying her was saving her from a life at Sheesh Mahal. During my imprisonment, Husna came several times to visit me when my father was out. I don't know how she managed that. But every time, she had a message and a meal for me. After a few weeks, I decided to run away. I discussed my plan with Husna and she agreed; I told her if she helped me, it might cost her her life, but she insisted.

'As soon as I got the chance, I escaped and went straight to Sheesh Mahal. I asked her mother for her hand. Her mother was hesitant, because she knew how a love like ours ended. She politely told me to forget her daughter. But I was stubborn. Aren't we all stubborn in love? Nevertheless, Mehr's mother was far more stubborn—women usually are. For two days, I lived at the brothel trying to convince her. But she was immovable. Finally, Husna came into the picture and begged her to let us marry. I don't know how Husna convinced her, but she agreed. And I married her immediately. We couldn't live at Sheesh Mahal after that, so I brought her to my house, thinking that my father would accept her, now that he didn't have a choice. But I was wrong. Mehr's mother had warned us about this— she had even tried to stop us—but I hadn't listened to her. I wish I had now.'

'Your father must have lost his mind when he—'

'He killed her.'

The imam looked at Moid, his eyes blank.

'I have seen the person who loved me the most killing the person I loved the most. He killed her because he thought he was better than her. He killed her because he thought she didn't deserve to be his daughter-in-law. He murdered her because he believed that he was pure, she was not. He killed her in his sheer arrogance, the same arrogance that turned an angel into the devil. He killed her because of his self-righteousness. He killed an innocent soul . . .'

'I am sorry . . .'

'Why are you sorry?' He smiled through the tears.

'For your loss . . .'

'It is the will of the One in whose hands my soul is . . .'

He saw the indecisiveness on the young man's face.

'Perhaps you want to ask me what happened next . . .'

Moid nodded.

'I lost all hope. I stopped eating, praying . . . living. But one day Husna visited me again. She gave me her condolences; I gave her mine. She said all the things that one is supposed to say to the husband who has lost his wife. But she didn't stop there. She told me that Mehr-un-Nisa had had a dream. She, who was born in a brothel, wanted to give women born into such conditions a new life, those who didn't have any source of income. She wanted to start a business embroidering women's salwar kameezes, and believed she could bring about a change with this. And then no woman would need to disgrace herself living a life she didn't want.

'Husna, knowingly or unknowingly, taught me that a lover could die but love couldn't. She, whose best friend had passed away because of me, gave me the strength to pick up my shattered pieces and make something beautiful out of it. As soon as I heard her speak, I knew what I had to do. I wanted to fulfil her dream, and Husna helped me do it. If I was the roof of that business, she was my pillar, and Mehr-un-Nisa was our foundation. Together we worked day and night. We supported each other. We became each other's shadow. We cradled each other. We cried together, we laughed together, we grew up together. And with us, her dream also grew. Now we support about five hundred women.'

He stopped and looked at Moid enquiringly.

'Will you tell her story to the world? I want the world to know that good and evil are not in mosques and brothels. It is in our hearts . . . I want people to stop killing Mehr-un-Nisa—again and again. I want them to look at their own sins . . .'

But before he could complete his sentence, somebody knocked on the door of the inner chamber.

'I am coming, Husna!' the old man said. 'She must have prepared the tea.'

The old man went outside and came back with two cups. He told Moid he had married Husna, that the universe had brought them together in this holy union. When they started their business, he had never thought that his wounds could heal. But Husna's support had strengthened him, healed him and her both. More than lovers they became companions who loved each other, who loved Mehr-un-Nisa together. He told Moid that they had decided to name their daughter after Mehr-un-Nisa, in honour of the lamp of love she had lit in their hearts.

Moid quietly listened to him and then took his leave. He had entered the masjid thinking he was doing humanity a favour by writing this book. But he was leaving as a different man—he was merely doing his job, and his job was to love. He now knew what true love was. Perhaps his dua had been answered. As he looked back at the masjid, a quote from Hafiz flashed through his mind:

Even after all this time, the sun never says to the earth, 'You owe me.' Look what happens with a love like that. It lights up the whole sky.

18

I Got You

Krusha Sahjwani Malkani

Anyone who has lived in India knows that love stories here are incomplete without a big fat wedding. Karan recalled the wedding day as if it were yesterday.

The visuals of the breathtaking decor, the flood of emotions running through him and the sound of the music and the voices were all so vivid in his mind. He had watched Kinjal walk down the stairs of the extravagantly decorated Udai Vilas. Her words still echoed in his ears, 'I will get married only in a Sabyasachi lehenga.' Karan remembered her babbling about this obsessive desire multiple times over the years that he had known and loved her. He never told her, but he had always believed that she would be the most beautiful woman in the room even if she walked out in her track pants and white tee. Especially if she walked out in her track pants and white tee.

It was a bright summer evening in June, which came with the promise of moisture between one's thighs rather than in one's eyes. But to everyone's surprise and relief, as they had gotten closer to the anointed hour, the wind gods had obliged and the evening had turned pleasantly breezy. Karan was not surprised by this, for he knew that Kinjal almost always had her way with the universe. The chapters she did not study never made it to the exam. The party she couldn't make always turned out to be no fun. It was only when they played cards that her luck would run out and Karan would emerge victorious.

Lucky in cards, unlucky in love, they say.

'I cannot find my left earring. It was here a second ago. I cannot get married like this! What will people say?' Kinjal had exclaimed in panic to her friends a few minutes before the big moment. Though she had spoken to all of them, her eyes had relied on Karan. She had grown used to depending on him. When she couldn't find her textbook a week before an exam, or when she had a fight with her mother or even if she was just craving Doritos, Karan had always been her first call.

'Then don't get married,' Karan had wanted to say, but, instead, he had just said, as he always did, 'Relax. I got you, Kinj.'

Little did he know that that was going to be the last time he said those words to her—for a few minutes later, she was married to Parth. And as the couple had vowed to love and cherish each other until death did them part, Karan had silently acknowledged the death of the only romantic love he had ever known. He had watched the orange of the sun slowly fade as the couple had publicly and religiously been declared husband and wife.

It had now been eighteen months since that day—when Kinjal had become someone else's wife—but Karan still thought of her on most days. The first two months had been the toughest. He was used to seeing her for coffee after work in the evenings, so he had to take up something else to fill that hour. He had opted for squash. He felt like it was a good way to release the negative energy he had pent up as well. It also took a lot of self-control for him to not reach for the phone to call her every time he had a free minute while in the Uber, or to not tag her every time he saw one of those hilarious cat videos he knew she loved.

With time though, it got slightly easier, but she never completely left his mind. Most days now it was just a passing thought, but some days the thoughts intensified. Like when he drank a few too many or when he watched *Friends*. Especially *that* episode. He had always believed she was his lobster. And sometimes he even closed his eyes and thought of her when he made love to his girlfriend, Amaya. But today was different. Today, thoughts of her were not like the regular background music in his day. He just could not shake her off his mind. It felt urgent. It felt like she was thinking of him too. Like she needed his help. And so, after avoiding the group chats and her missed calls for all these months, he decided to call her.

The plan was to just hear her voice, find out if she was okay and then hang up and claim it was a butt-dial. But she did not answer. He didn't know her schedule any more. She was probably just busy. Maybe she was in dance class. Did she still go to those? Maybe she was in the kitchen. It broke his heart a little to picture her cooking. She had never liked to cook, and she was quite lousy at it. She couldn't even make Maggi well. That was always Karan's duty. Then again, she probably had a large staff to order around now. Worse yet, maybe after all the unexplained avoiding that he had been doing over the past year, she probably just did not want to speak to him any more. And ordinarily, he would have let it go but something was different today.

He had this growing pit in his stomach, which, despite not eating a morsel all morning, made him feel like he was going to throw up.

He called a common friend, Nisha, and asked her to call Kinjal. To his relief, she did not probe him as much as he had thought she might. Everyone was clearly a lot busier for this kind of stuff than they used to be in college. She just casually informed him that Kinjal and her husband had gone to Gir forest for the long weekend, which was probably why she was not answering calls. That explanation should have sufficed.

'Could you please call her husband, Nisha? It will only take a minute. I just want to know that she's okay.' The words spilt out of him without a thought.

That invited the probing. Karan struggled to explain why it was so important for him to get through to Kinjal right now. He did not really understand it himself, so it was in vain that he tried to put it into words. And so, after a failed attempt at doing so, he hung up. He decided to distract himself till the gnawing feeling left him. He tried reading a book that lay next to his bed. Artificial intelligence and the world of marketing. He had read only ten pages in a month. That clearly wasn't the right distraction to fall back on. Karan had never been much of a reader. The only book he had read up to the last word was some romance novel that Kinjal had forced on him. The over-the-top romantic gestures, the big weddings and the tragic endings had all been too much for him. Of course, he had known that even before he started the book, but saying no to Kinjal had never been his forte.

Since the bedside book had failed him, he switched on the television. After spending minutes trying to decide on what to watch on Netflix, he gave up and started pacing the room. Eventually, he decided to call Parth himself. He knew he was probably overreacting, but he just needed to know that she was all right. So much so that he was ready to put himself through this awkward call. Karan did not care much for small talk and had managed to stay out of Parth's way ever since he had met him at the engagement. They had barely exchanged ten words since. Kinjal had pushed Karan to make a bigger attempt but he had always blown her off with some joke like, 'Are you marrying him or me? Do you want me to take him out for coffee too?' He wondered if Parth even had his number stored.

'The number you have called is currently switched off.'

People switched off their phones on vacation. Forests often did not have network or charging points. All plausible reasons. But Karan's feeling of panic began manifesting itself physically now, in the form of an incoming anxiety attack. He had never experienced one before this. He just had to make it stop, and so all his inhibitions flew out of the window. He decided to call Kinjal's mother, hoping her number had not changed.

If there was ever one person who would know where Kinjal was at all times, it was her. And even if Karan did not know Kinjal's schedule any more, he was sure this was something that marriage would not have changed.

'Hello? Karan?'

She had answered!

'Hi, Aunty. I am sorry to bother you. I wanted something urgently from Kinjal. I know she is in Gir, but any chance you have spoken to her this morning? I was trying to reach her . . .'

'No, beta. I have been trying to reach her myself, but she has not answered since morning. Maybe she has gone for the safari or something.'

Karan felt like he was choking but managed to say, 'No problem, Aunty. I will speak to her later.'

Something just did not feel right. Maybe it was the anxiety, but it felt like crippling thoughts were placing themselves one on top of the other in his mind, like in a game of Jenga—and that it was only moments before something tugged at the wrong piece and it all came crashing down.

He opened her Instagram account. No new stories. It was very unlike her to not post anything while travelling. He needed a better distraction. She was scheduled to be home tomorrow, as per Nisha, so he just needed to pass the day without doing anything stupid, but his mind was not cooperating.

We all have certain moments in life when we are magnetically drawn to do something without any logical explanation to justify it. And so, with a heaving chest, Karan sat in front of his laptop and, with trembling fingers, typed

'Gir forest' and chose the news section. Anyone would have thought he was crazy. But a moment later, he really wished he were. He wished he was hallucinating and that his eyes were deceiving him due to his paranoia.

A young couple dies on the spot in a jeep accident . . .

He did not even need to read it further. There weren't any names disclosed at this point, but he just knew. He tried to go through the rest of the article, reading through his tears.

Hours later, a call from a flabbergasted Nisha confirmed the news. He had not moved from his spot since he had first read the article. He did not call anyone to inform them, because there were no confirmed names and he knew the news would reach them all soon. He saw no reason to bring them pain before it was time. In any case, he felt paralysed from the anguish.

Nisha rambled on about how she could not believe his feeling had been right, but her voice had just become noise to him by this point, like the creaking fan or the buzzing insect in the room.

~

The next few months passed in agony. People sympathize with you when you lose a friend, but they put a limit to the acceptable threshold and length of your pain. If you lose a child or a parent or a spouse, then the rules are different. But Karan was not the husband. He was not permitted to grieve the way he wanted to. He had already acknowledged the death of his love once at Kinjal's wedding and he had fought through it by telling himself that the worst was over. If only he had known. After the wedding, her social media had at least given him a glimpse into her life and reaffirmed to him that she was happy—but now he yearned to feel her presence. He had not known a world without her in his entire adult life.

Six months later, he sat in front of the television, watching *that* episode of *Friends* for the first time since the dreadful news. And he watched his phone accidentally dial her number. No one would have believed him or understood it, but it did not matter. He knew she was visiting. And so, he went and brought her favourite fuzzy blanket and made two bowls of Maggi. One with more cheese and less schezwan, just as she liked it.

And then he whispered, 'I got you, Kinj.'

19

The Other Side of the Road

Hamsini R.

Rashi tapped her pen impatiently on her desk. She was looking at her book through sleepy, unfocused eyes. It was the last period of the day and the bell was taking an inordinately long time to ring. Uninterested in the lesson, she furtively glanced to her left. Rajat sat a few rows ahead of her, staring at the blackboard like his future was laid out on it.

'It probably is,' she thought, smirking to herself. Studious boys like him never missed a day of school and filled their copies with endless notes. She watched his ink pen fly across the page, fascinated by his tiny, cramped handwriting, barely visible at this distance. She smiled to herself when he wrinkled his nose to adjust his glasses for the umpteenth time.

'Is there something funny you want to share with the class, Rashi?' her teacher asked sarcastically.

Everyone turned to look at her. Catching Rajat's eye, a warm flush rose to her cheeks. She murmured a quick sorry and trained her eyes back on the book.

She risked a look at him again. His fingers were unconsciously tapping his 'Class Leader' badge pinned to his shirt. The small window between classes, when he would stand in the front of the class, was her favourite time. She would talk loudly to her friends, trying to attract as much attention to herself as possible. Invariably, he would notice her and give her a warning look.

'Rashi, please don't make noise or I will write your name on the board.'

'Go ahead, I don't care,' she would reply defiantly, daring him to pick up the chalk and write her name. He would sigh angrily and write her name on the 'disruptive students' list. That moment of interaction was always worth the inevitable punishment.

When the bell finally rang, Rashi packed her bag slowly. Maybe today was the day she would work up the nerve to ask Rajat for his science notes. It was the perfect excuse to talk to him. She walked towards where he was still seated, his elbow propped up on the desk, chin resting in his open palm.

'Er . . . ahem!' She cleared her throat noisily. Just as she was about to ask for his notes, he turned around and looked at her. His dark eyes, complemented by a charming, cute face, had a puzzled expression in them. She was momentarily speechless and forgot what she wanted to ask him.

'Do you want me to move my bag?' he asked, pointing towards his abnormally large book bag with two buckles straining against the sheer number of textbooks in it.

'Yeah, how can anyone walk to the door if your bag is blocking the way? What do you bring in this anyway? Rocks?' She arched an eyebrow at him.

She winced. What happened to asking for his notes nicely?

'It was a simple yes-or-no question,' he said.

She was still debating asking for his notes when he quietly picked his bag up and walked out. Great, now she had hurt his feelings. She followed him out of the classroom and walked towards the cycle shed, where her friends were discussing summer holidays, just a few weeks away.

'How can anyone carry this bag of rocks out of this shed if you're blocking the way?' Rajat asked with a twinkle in his eye. Smirking, Rashi moved out of his way. He unlocked his cycle and left the shed.

She waved to her friends and unlocked the shiny new BSA Ladybird her father had given her for her birthday. She had insisted that a cycle was the only thing she wanted that year. It had nothing to do with the fact that the cycle would give her a few more minutes with Rajat in the cycle shed. Of course not.

Outside the school gate, she was about to pedal away when a movement caught her eye. She spotted the familiar lopsided white socks, navy blue trousers and white shirt. Rajat was on the opposite side of the road, trying to strap his oversized bag on to the tiny backseat of his slightly rusty Atlas bicycle.

Intensely aware of his presence, Rashi pushed her cycle forward. The road stretched between them comfortably, giving her the space she needed to steady herself on the handlebars before she resolutely marched ahead, resisting the temptation to look at him. She counted to ten, knowing that by then he would have started pedalling, and looked across the road. With a pleasant jolt, she realized he was pushing his cycle on the other side of the road, parallel to hers.

Tiny goosebumps sprouted on her arms, defying the May sun. She smiled to herself when his voice snapped her out of her reverie.

'Why are you pushing your cycle?' he asked.

She considered his question. When nothing rational came to mind, she chose to reply with a question of her own. 'Why are you pushing yours?' she asked.

He didn't respond and they walked in companionable silence for the next few minutes.

'Do you live nearby?' she ventured.

'Yes.' His monosyllabic response came swiftly.

After some time, Rashi saw the familiar fork in the road that led to her house. She sneaked a peek and saw him pushing his cycle farther down the other road in the fork. Reluctantly, she took the turn to her house, watching him walk away.

The next day, her name was on the blackboard, as usual. She smiled at his handwriting hugging her name in chalk letters. After classes, she left for the cycle shed and pushed it to the gate, waving to her friends.

Her mind registered his presence before her eyes noticed the glint of his perfectly white shirt gleaming in the hot sun. They walked in complete silence, on opposite sides of the road, till it was time for her to take the eventual turn to her house. She had no idea why neither of them pedalled—but there they were, day after day, pushing the damn things on their own sides of the road. It was the best part of her day.

One evening, her parents were unusually sombre, as if trying to break bad news to her. After dinner, her father motioned her to sit down.

'Rashi beta, do you remember when we moved here five years ago?' her father asked her gently.

She nodded, not sure what this was about.

'Well, I have received my transfer orders to move to Pune next month. I tried pushing it by a year, but this year the transfer is inevitable. We have to apply for school admissions when we get there, find a place to live, there's a lot to do . . .' Her dad trailed off at the stricken look on Rashi's face.

'Papa, I like my school. I'm doing better in my studies here. Can't we stay?' she pleaded. But she knew it was hopeless. Her father couldn't refuse a transfer order any more than she could avoid moving with them. It was the nature of her father's job. They had been moving to a new city every few years. She knew the drill. She usually welcomed the grand adventure in a new city. But this move was different. She didn't want to leave here. Her stomach felt hollow.

The weeks soon dwindled into days and the last day of school arrived.

Rashi dragged her feet to school. She had told all her friends about her move, taking their numbers, promising to be in touch. She hadn't quite figured out how to tell him and, more importantly, ask for his phone number.

She looked back at the freshly wiped blackboard, where her name used to be. There was an air of excited anticipation in class, which did not match her sombre demeanour.

She watched the back of his head from her usual seat. Determined to do *something,* she hurriedly tore a piece of paper from her notebook and wrote in it. She crumpled it into a ball and threw it as hard as she could towards him.

It hit him square on his back. He straightened up and looked down at the chit of paper. Puzzled, he opened it.

Can you meet me at the cycle shed? I want to talk to you.

—*Rashi*

He turned to look at her and flashed a quick thumbs up.

There, the first hurdle was done. Now if only she could muster up the courage to ask him for his number.

'I *will* ask him!' Rashi thought, steeling herself.

The last day of the school year finally ended to much cheer. Everyone tore out of the classroom, running out to greet the holidays with the respect it deserved.

Walking towards the cycle shed, Rashi hadn't the faintest idea about how to start the conversation. Rajat walked in just then, unlocking his cycle. Without saying a word, they pushed their cycles together in step, only this time on the same side of the road.

'So . . .' they both began together.

'G-go ahead,' Rashi stammered, blushing.

'I heard you are moving to Pune,' Rajat said, looking at her forehead.

'Er, yeah. Dad got transferred. We are moving in a week,' she replied.

'Oh, okay,' he said, uncharacteristically quiet.

'Rajat?' She looked at him. 'Can you give me your phone number? I'll call once I reach Pune.' It was a rushed sentence.

He stopped in the middle of the road. She came to a halt beside him.

'Give me your notebook,' he said.

Rashi handed him her school diary and watched with quiet excitement as he scribbled his landline number on the last page. He handed it back to her and she carefully kept it back in her bag.

They reached the eventual fork in the road and stood there for a long time, smiling at each other. Rajat seemed to want to say something, but changed his mind, happy to just stand there and watch her walk away.

The next few weeks were a blur of moving vans and settling in an unfamiliar city. When they finally installed the telephone line, she ran to her room, tearing open the boxes that had her school things. She searched through two boxes full of her belongings but couldn't find the diary.

'Ma! Did you see my diary from the last school?' she yelled out from her room.

'It should be among your boxes. Look again,' her mother yelled back.

Rashi turned her room upside down, searching every unopened or half-opened box. Her parents watched bemused as she dashed from one room to another, trying to find the elusive diary. She couldn't find it even after several hours of intense destruction of her room. Dejected and tired, she plopped to the floor.

'Ma, did you see it while unpacking? I had all my friends' numbers in that diary,' she asked weakly.

'I'll help you look for it,' her mother said, gently stroking her hair.

Over the next few days, her mother helped her search every nook and cranny, but the diary never made an appearance. It seemed well and truly lost in the move.

Rashi felt a sharp pain of disappointment in her chest. She sat in her room, moodily looking at her newly wrapped notebooks, quiet tears trailing down her face.

Five years later . . .

Rashi was scrolling through her Orkut scraps, the concave monitor giving her a headache. In college, she was finally able to persuade her parents to buy her a computer for her room so she didn't have to go to the cybercafé down the road every time she had an assignment due.

Just as she was about to call it a day, she noticed a notification indicating a new chat message. No sooner had she clicked on the message than her heart started hammering loudly in her chest at the familiar name and display photo.

'Hello, Ms Talkative. This is Rajat Desai. The boy who wrote your name on the blackboard and got you into trouble all through ninth standard.'

'Hi, Class Leader. Still taking rocks to college?' she replied, fingers flying on the keyboard in her hurry to reply to him.

'It has been a while! What college are you in?' he enquired.

'I'm in Fergusson, studying literature. What about you?' she typed back.

'I'm studying Mech at IIT Delhi.' he responded.

'Some things have remained consistent, I see,' she typed back, smiling.

He was still adorably studious.

They chatted for a while, exchanging pleasantries about college majors and the simplicity of school life. They reminisced about their teachers and how much they missed homework compared to the atrocities of college assignments. Rashi relaxed in her chair. Conversation with him was surprisingly easy.

After a while, she looked at the time and groaned.

'Okay, I have to log off now. My parents will blow a fuse if they see me on the computer for too long,' she said, reluctant to log off but not wanting to give her parents an excuse to catch her late at night. She waited for him to wish her goodnight and log off. He was still typing.

A few moments later, the screen filled up with his words.

'Why didn't you call, Rashi? I waited for months for the phone to ring.'

Rashi took a deep breath and closed her eyes.

'I wanted to, believe me. I lost the school diary that had everyone's numbers in it. I turned the house upside down looking for it. I never found it.'

'Oh, okay,' he typed back.

'I really wanted to, Rajat. Without any numbers or addresses handy, I couldn't stay in touch with anyone. I was miserable that entire year,' she replied, hesitant.

'Yeah, I was bummed too.'

'Why were you waiting for my call?' she asked boldly.

It was ten minutes before he replied. She thought he had left the chat.

'Will it be too awkward to tell you now that I had a huge crush on you in school? I don't know if you knew, but I pushed my cycle in the opposite direction to my house every single day just so I could walk with you.'

Rashi stared at the message on the screen for a long time.

The screen flashed a new message.

'Are you there?'

Her fingers shaking, she typed her reply and hit enter.

' . . . I had a crush on you too. I pushed the cycle so I could walk with you.'

☺

☺

She felt a familiar smile tugging at the corners of her mouth, a new feeling blooming in her chest that she couldn't quite name.

20

Something in the Rain

Kaustubhi Singh

I wanted to wake up thinking, believing, that my life was finally on track. I wasn't the last person wishing for this, but I wanted sanity—and I wanted closure.

I am twenty-five and was diagnosed with chronic alcoholism about three months ago—and it wasn't a problem until my ex-fiancé's wife reported me for threatening them. I hadn't been clean for this long—fifty-five days in a row, with minimal withdrawal symptoms—but my anxiety was still pretty bad, so the rehab doctors decided to give me counselling, and I was in no position to deny. My withdrawal symptoms from alcohol weren't as painful as the ones from heartbreak. They were more to deal with, and that is why I started drinking in the first place—to avoid the ache in my chest that felt like a rotting tooth.

I take a little walk in my cubicle for one last time because I'll be given a clearance today. I sit on the brown wooden chair I used to kick when I was so miserable that the doctors had to tie my hands up. Alcohol was my escape. The idea of alcohol was not pleasure but an escape, because when that warm liquor burns your throat, it starts dissolving the hurt stuck down there and slowly numbs you so you don't feel the hurt. Heartbreak isn't beautiful; it isn't some literature; it's not listening to sad songs or something like that. It's feeling okay for a minute and then starting to feel their ghost around you, their touch on your skin. You miss them, you miss them so much that you choke on your memories with them.

Dr Mayank Sharma, my shrink, almost my age, tells me that it will always hurt, and it will make one cry and scream till one's nose is blocked and eyes puffy; that hurt is inevitable but it will hurt less, and I will see and understand why someone did what they did. And I think I understand. When I look back to the day Robbie left me for another woman, he said he had grown out of love and I stood there thinking: Where did I go wrong? But thinking about it now makes me realize I did everything to truly belong to Robbie. I changed myself for him, I changed my ways and choices for him when I should have let him love me for who I was, because that's what love is, that's what love is supposed to be—loving someone for who they are.

Dr Mayank also says that love is ironic—it lets you cage your older self in and metamorphose into someone new. And I agree, but if the changes aren't letting you become a better person, what use is it then?

My thoughts are disrupted by someone's approaching footsteps. I tilt my head to see who it is, but in my heart

I know it's Dr Mayank. He has helped me a lot; he has seen me going to extremes and only he had the calm to cool me down. And, honestly, from the past week, whenever he is around I feel comfortable and relaxed, like I'm home.

'How are you, Anjali?' His voice is calm and deep.

I stand up so he can sit on the chair. 'I'm good, doctor,' I smile.

Sometimes I smile on purpose because I'm kind of attracted to him. He has never judged me, but that's what shrinks do—listen without judging. I'm thankful my sessions started last month, because it would have been terrible to face him after knowing he has seen me beg for alcohol.

'Last day . . . Hmm . . .' He opens my file. 'I'm impressed with your recovery. You're a great patient. I'm so proud of you!' He signs on the yellow file.

'I'm happy I'm clean.' I finally sit on the bed.

'So . . . Anything you want to talk about with your shrink one last time?' He smiles and I can't help but notice how beautifully two small dimples form under his bottom lip. I want to laugh at myself for looking at him like that.

'I want closure, doctor. One last time, I want to close my eyes and replay the last year and never look back again,' I admit.

He pulls his chair closer to me so he can hold my hand, and I wonder if it's okay for him to do that. He gives me a soft nod and I close my eyes.

I take a deep breath before speaking. 'When Robbie asked me to marry him, I said we were too young, but then he hugged me and told me we were supposed to be together. I was so in love that I agreed, until I found out four months after our unofficial engagement that he was sleeping with someone else. I felt like I was sinking and that there wasn't enough oxygen in the air to keep me alive. He started to hurt me with his words and actions, and I never knew how evil he could get until he took pride in what he did to me.'

He gently circles the back of my hand with his thumb, and for the first time I don't feel like crying.

I take a breath again. 'I thought I could end the hurt by drinking, but whenever I was sober, I could feel the clouds of sorrow build up again—so I drank again. I tried to escape this hurt. I was so mad that I invested so much in him but he decided to give his love to another woman. I used to drink and call him. God, I used to call him till he picked up the phone and shattered my heart again, but even then I didn't feel ashamed. I wanted to be humiliated so that it would trigger my self-esteem and help me move on.'

'It's okay, Anjali, you're in a very good position now.' His voice felt warm and homely.

'There's more,' I grin and continue, 'I used to apologize a lot. I used to wake up and say sorry and check my phone, because I knew I must have screwed up again. I lost my job, I lost everything—I lost myself. One day I got to know that Robbie and Simran had had a baby, so I just wanted to wish them. I showed up at their place and his wife thought I was going to harm them, so she reported me.'

I sigh. 'I'm happy she did, Mayank. I'm glad she did.' I open my eyes and he smiles—maybe he is smiling at how I addressed him without the prefix 'doctor'.

'Sometimes . . . sometimes, Anjali, things don't just break—they shatter and the unexpected happens, and you get hurt by someone you trusted more than your life. But grief doesn't change you, it reveals you,' he says and I catch the last line.

'It's from *The Fault in Our Stars*, right? The last line?' I manage a smile.

'Yes, I see you're very sharp too.' He laughs. 'So who is coming to pick you up?'

'My mom.'

He grabs the file again. 'I see you live like just ten minutes from here.'

'Yeah.'

A guard comes and tells him that my mother is there. He waits for me until I pick up my belongings.

My mom looks young and I hug her when I see her.

'Mrs Seth, nice to meet you. I'm your daughter's shrink, Mayank.' He shakes hands with Mom.

'Is she fine?' she asks.

'Yes, your daughter is completely fine. Just make sure she takes her medicines properly.'

He hands her his clinical notes and my file. I smile at him, thinking this is the last time I will see this man who had helped me get through my own miserable mind—or maybe I will see him again someday with someone and I will remember how grateful I am for him.

'Come, Anjali, let's go. Thank you, doctor,' my mom says.

'Take this, Anjali. This is my card. If anything happens, please call me.'

He gives me his visiting card, and I give him a smile.

My mom arranges a house-warming party for my welcome but I honestly don't think it's necessary, because the reason I went to rehab is embarrassing and unfortunate. But she says, 'It's only a little happiness that matters.' She is happy that I am clean but I still have a feeling that she is disturbed by the actions I took in the past. When you go through a process, you hurt everyone who cares and loves you, and I hurt her.

'I'm going to get a shower and change.' I go straight to my room. For the first time, I feel like a stranger in my own room.

I wear a pink-and-white floral dress and open the drawer to grab some clips. I see my phone lying there. I haven't used my phone since I got into rehab, because they want the people there to engage in physical activities and not digital—and it had worked because I don't even want to switch it on any more. But I do.

'I'll save Dr Mayank's number,' I think to myself and long-press the power button. The first message that pops up is Robbie's.

I'm sorry, Anjali. Simran shouldn't have done that. I'm sorry.

I read it and I keep my phone back in. I shut my eyes and open them again, trying to avoid any unwanted thoughts. I brush my hair and keep biting the inside of my cheek to avoid any sort of breakdown. I don't want to let people down any more; I've done enough damage.

'Oh my baby!' Minne Aunty hugs me and kisses my cheek. I look around, and there are only three people in the room—that, too, Mom's friends. I'm not disappointed that she didn't call mine, because I don't have any. Everyone I know is linked to Robbie. I sit near Minne Aunty and a nostalgic smell hits my nostrils—liquor. My hands start to shiver and my neck tickles. I feel like I'm going to go crazy. I get up and walk to the window, and I feel a hand on my shoulder. I look back and see it's Mayank.

'As a doctor, I can't be prouder.' He pats my back and I just smile. I'm too preoccupied with the nausea building up inside me. 'So, if I take you out, will you come?' he says, and I just look at him like he's some ghost, and he waits for me to say something.

'Isn't it against the . . . er, rules or something?' I try to regain my senses.

'No, I'm here as a guy asking a gorgeous girl out,' he says.

Mom allows me to go out. She thinks it's therapy, but I grab this opportunity to look forward to life. I realize I am not the only one noticing him around. He takes me to an ice-cream hub.

'I think it's going to pour,' he says while locking the car.

'I think I should buy my favourite flavour for you, and you buy me yours.' I smile and he nods. I choose cookie crème for him and he selects mint chocolate for me.

'Why did you ask me out on a date?' We are sitting near the balcony area under the pink umbrella.

'It's a treat. You passed your test. You didn't touch it even though you got the withdrawal symptoms.'

I feel embarrassed for referring to it as a date. He says he likes the flavour I got for him but I feel like his is better. It's minty and sweet, probably my favourite from now on, but I don't want to tell him that and feel embarrassed again. This man knows everything about me and I just know his name and what he does.

'How old are you?' I finally ask.

'Twenty-six.' He pauses and adds with a laugh, 'Unmarried.' I smile because I think it will be weird if I don't. Doctors do have a weird sense of humour.

'I really like the person you are. Your presence makes me feel something I've never felt, and you're pretty too, so I just thought, you know . . .' He raises his shoulders. How can he say something like that so easily? Then I remember that he's trained—he's a shrink.

'Beauty is a myth.'

'The soul is timeless,' he says. 'I don't choose you for your history, I chose you for you.'

'Why do bad things happen to good people?' I finish my cup of ice cream.

'Because if bad things happened to bad people, it would be a good thing,' he says and I laugh. 'I should capture this— a happy you—and maintain a record.' He starts tapping his pockets. 'I think I left it in the car. I'll just get it.' He leaves.

I look around and see a familiar face approaching me, and my heartbeat goes crazy.

'Hi, Anjali.' Robbie waves at me. He waits for me to say something but I don't—I just look down and think about how bad my luck is. 'I heard about you. I'm so sorry. We didn't mean to. I hope you're good now.' His words are harsh and I want to get up and leave, but I don't— I want to face it. I feel like a rebel in my own body.

'It's okay. I'm great.' I force a smile.

'I was worried. I hope you're over it,' he says and gets under the umbrella, since it has started drizzling.

I feel my legs freezing up. 'I'm over you. Actually, I'm here with someone.'

His expression changes like he's mad at me, and then he looks up.

'Should we leave, honey?' Mayank's hand feels warm on my cold body, and I nod.

'Hi, I'm Robbie.' Robbie extends his hand and Mayank takes it.

'I'm Mayank.' He smiles.

'You're with her?' he asks him like he cares.

'Yeah, heard a lot about you, though. I'm a professional, so it's a little out of line, but you seriously suck for messing with her. She's a gem,' he says, and grabs my hand. I keep looking at him as we leave.

'Stand here.' Mayank takes out his phone.

'It's drizzling,' I say, so that he doesn't click but he does.

'A woman like you should be kept safe. All the things you like about yourself and everything you don't should be kept safe to make you realize the person you are and the person you're becoming.'

He smiles and I quietly start to walk towards the car with him. I can't stop replaying it all in my head and blushing. I am not sure when it happened but I feel something, some way, when I am around Mayank, like we are connected and all I can do now is pray that he feels the same way. I grab his hand; he doesn't look back. But I know . . . I know something has happened. Something has happened in the rain, and I'm not letting go.

21

A Tender Ray of Love

Nandita Warrier

She was three; he was five. He found her silly; she found him bossy. Their mothers were soul sisters. So their families met often.

She was six; he was eight. He found her irritating and called her a 'complaint box'; she found him obnoxious and called him a 'monster'. They fought in every get-together.

She was nine; he was eleven. He found her intelligent but boring; she found him incredibly cute and funny.

She was twelve; he was fourteen. He secretly detested her scholarly attitude; she was swept by his charm and wrote about him in her secret diary.

She was fifteen; he was seventeen. He just couldn't connect with the bookworm she had become and ran out of topics whenever they met; she was head over heels in love with this dashing young lad—chirpy, energetic, popular, confident and so much more. Boy, she could've given a limb for his attention.

She was eighteen; he was twenty. She aspired to be a doctor; he was determined to be one of the 'Men in Blue'.

Their paths were growing apart, just like their personalities. They rarely met, and when they did, she was more awkward than before. He didn't seem interested in her and she was torn whether or not to share her feelings with him.

And then something happened. He did something terrible—unforgivable! She had held him in such high regard all along, loved him with all her heart, but he had treated her like trash. She was shattered.

But instead of confronting him, she chose to remain silent. What was the point of hurting herself even more?

From that day, she studiously avoided him.

She was twenty-four; he was twenty-six. She was a doctor, preparing for MD. Over the years, she'd become more self-assured and cheerful. He was a disillusioned Ranji player, stuck playing for his state. Over the years, his confidence and drive had seen a steady dip.

She was twenty-seven; he was twenty-nine. She was a bright, young surgeon winning people over; he was a lost and bitter soul, spewing venom at everyone.

She was twenty-eight; he was thirty. She was full of dreams; he was broken.

That night, she slept early because she had a morning duty in the ICU. That night, he slept late after emptying a bottle of sleeping pills.

Just as Ramya reached the hospital, she was summoned to the OT for an emergency procedure. 'Suicide attempt,' someone whispered. Dr Iyer was instructing the team when Ramya joined them in her OT scrubs. She threw a casual look at the patient and immediately recoiled. It was Rohan! Oh no, how could this be? Memories from her childhood, locked away in some corner, defiantly barged in, making her want to sob.

He looked so pale and pitiable—a mere shadow of the handsome young man she remembered from their last meeting years back! Rohan had had everything going for him—what could have possibly gone so wrong? Sensing her discomfort, Dr Iyer enquired, 'You know him?'

'Family friend,' she uttered nonchalantly, hiding the wave of sadness sweeping over her.

Once Rohan was resuscitated, Dr Iyer assigned his case to Ramya. 'He needs emotional support more than medical care. You can help his family deal with the situation—they seem comfortable with you.'

'BUT I AM NOT COMFORTABLE WITH THIS CASE!' she wanted to shout. 'I HAVE TAKEN YEARS TO GET OVER THIS MAN. DO YOU HAVE ANY IDEA HOW PAINFUL ONE-SIDED LOVE IS? AND I STILL HAVEN'T GOTTEN OVER WHAT HE DID. PLEASE SPARE ME!'

Instead, she took the case papers from Dr Iyer with a nod and made a resolve: 'No room for the past. As a doctor, I'll do my best.'

~

'So how are we today?' Ramya smiled enthusiastically. Rohan turned the other way without responding. This was becoming a routine, but Ramya wasn't going to give up so easily.

Outside the room, she met his worried mother. 'Rohan has lost all will to live. I'm afraid he'll do something again as soon as we go home.'

'Aunty, our resident psychiatrist, Dr Awasthi, will discharge Rohan only when he is emotionally stable. Don't worry,' Ramya assured her.

After her duty hours, when Ramya went to check on Rohan, his mother looked unwell. Out of concern, she touched the old woman's forehead. 'Oh God, Aunty, you're running a high fever. You must go home and rest.' She also got her a paracetamol and checked her vitals.

'I will, beta, after Rohan's brother relieves me. He'll be here around 10.'

Ramya protested. 'Mom will kill me if I allow you to stay here in this condition. Don't worry, I'll manage.'

After much cajoling, the old woman was escorted home and Ramya sat next to Rohan, well anchored by her sense of duty.

'You used to be so bossy, always trying to control me,' she complained.

Rohan ignored her.

'Don't you remember?' she persisted.

Rohan gave her an irritated look. 'What are you talking about?'

'Of course you know what I am talking about.' A mischievous smile danced upon her lips. Ramya had decided to use childhood memories to break the ice. 'Even in Snakes & Ladders, you used to decide all the rules.'

'I never made any rules; I only explained them to you,' he said point-blank.

Happy that he had taken the bait, Ramya prodded on, 'Really? I thought you conveniently twisted them to your advantage.'

'That is so not true! Controlling maybe, for you were a silly little girl who knew nothing. But manipulating?' He sat up and looked straight at her.

Ramya explained, 'I clearly remember that when you got a six, you would get a bonus chance—but not me!'

'That's because if six points take you to a snake, you don't get a bonus,' he clarified.

For the first time in all these days, Rohan looked engaged. She was relieved at the ease of their conversation.

'Kudos! You still remember the rules,' Ramya laughed.

'Kudos to you—for remembering minor details from a quarter-century back, and also for your confidence in the recall!' His eyes shone with sarcasm. And he was almost ready to smile. She continued the mock fight and, soon, they were pulling each other's leg, remembering funny incidents—some embarrassing ones too.

'Childhood is so pure, so complete. I wish I could go back to the good old days.' Rohan sighed.

'Pure? Yes, absolutely.' Ramya squirmed, controlling her emotions.

This was a big shift for Rohan. From not wanting to live, not wishing for anything at all, he was longing for something, albeit from his childhood. Something was alive!

~

Rohan's mother's illness kept her at home. His brother could chip in only after office hours. So a big part of Rohan's responsibility came to Ramya. Dr Iyer understood that the patient needed support, so Ramya started visiting Rohan whenever possible.

'Do you want to step out to the terrace?' she asked one evening.

'Terrace? I didn't know we had access to one here.' Rohan smiled.

'Yeah, they didn't want you to know,' Ramya blurted out and immediately bit her lip.

'I get that. Don't worry,' Rohan assured her.

It was November and a cool breeze welcomed them as they walked out. Carrying their coffee, they settled in a corner. 'Remember we used to play hide-and-seek on your terrace?' Ramya reminisced.

Rohan nodded with a tiny smile and looked far away. Gathering all her courage, Ramya asked, 'What happened to you, Rohan?'

The concern in her voice travelled straight to his heart.

'There was nothing to look forward to, Ramya. Ever since I can remember, I had only one dream—to play for India. I was so focused on it that the rest of my life became a blur. But, slowly, my dream started slipping out of my hands. Still, I kept giving myself hope. One day, even hope refused to hold my hand; nobody wants to stand with a failure.'

Not knowing what to say, Ramya listened. And Rohan poured out his disappointment, anger—and tears. Somehow, he wasn't embarrassed or ashamed. With Ramya, he felt safe . . . and understood.

They had no idea when the golden sky turned orange, then pink, then grey—and finally black.

~

Ramya was in a spin—part of her hated Rohan and wanted to punish him. Another part went further back, constantly reminding her of the tenderness she had once felt for him. Much to her horror, a tiny flicker of that emotion still touched her. And then there was a third part that wanted her to fulfil her duty and just move on.

If there was one thing she felt certain about, it was her need for closure. After all, she wasn't that timid, fearful girl any more, lacking the courage to speak up! Her decision to stay silent had not allowed her to move on in life. Neither was she at peace with Rohan, nor was she able to trust other men completely. The few relationships she'd had couldn't blossom since she always held herself back.

About time she sorted things out, Ramya decided. But she understood that Rohan was still in recovery, and it wouldn't be right to disturb that. Once stable, he would have some explaining to do.

~

'What is this?' Rohan looked at the packet in Ramya's hands.

'Something you'll enjoy, I'm sure.' She grinned.

And with the excitement of a five-year-old, she pulled out a game of Snakes & Ladders.

'Are you serious?' He laughed.

'Of course, but this time I will make the rules.'

Only after Rohan promised to play did she reveal the rules. 'Every time we hit a snake, we will talk about a mistake and what we've learnt from it. And every time we reach a ladder, we will talk of a blessing and how it supports us. Rest of the rules are as before.'

Stunned for a moment, Rohan wanted to crawl back into his shell. But he reminded himself that Ramya was only being helpful. This could be cathartic, for all he knew! He hesitantly agreed and, once the game started, slowly began enjoying it. Before long, they were both accessing private corners of their hearts, revealing what had been fiercely guarded from the world. And when the biggest snake bit Rohan, moving him from 97 to 13, he not only spoke about the suicide attempt as his biggest mistake but also promised to never go on that path.

'I've learnt how deeply I'm loved. People stood by me even when I abandoned myself. I won't let them down again.'

Ramya was moved by the pain in his voice. Instinctively, she reached out and touched his arm. It felt nice, surprisingly nice—warm and reassuring, to both of them.

~

Dr Awasthi was quite pleased with Rohan's progress and gave instructions for his discharge the next day. Ramya rushed to share the good news and Rohan was ready to celebrate.

'Coffee on the terrace?'

She gladly agreed and soon they were sitting in their usual spot, paper cups in hand, breeze in their hair.

'I had never thought that I would come to love this syrupy coffee so much.' Rohan laughed, but Ramya seemed lost in her own thought. Clearing his throat, Rohan continued, 'You know, these coffee conversations have helped me heal at so many levels. I was so focused on my failure that I had lost all sense of possibilities. The childhood memories reconnected me with who I really am.'

Taking a pause, Rohan sipped on some coffee and glanced at Ramya. Immediately, his expression softened out of affection for this lovely girl whom he had never valued before. 'You shared so many incidents with me, Ramya, always painting me as the hero! It helped me view myself differently—someone with a lot of promise, talent and blessings. This is who I am, even today. I just need to believe this and create a new dream! How can I ever thank you for bringing the spark back?'

Rohan looked at her with such tenderness that she felt unsettled.

But Ramya had made up her mind—now or never!

'You know what, Rohan? I didn't paint you as a hero—I truly believed you were one. And you knew that I hero-worshipped you, didn't you?'

Oblivious to what was brewing inside her, Rohan nodded.

'Is that why you called me a pet poodle, always wagging my tail at you?' Her tone changed, and so did their expressions. 'Is that why you read the secrets from my diary and made fun of me in front of your friends?'

Ramya's face went red with anger while Rohan's face was white like ash.

'Is that why you bragged to your friends that you could have me any day—just that I wasn't your type?'

Rohan sat with his head in his hands, too ashamed to look at Ramya. Eventually, when he found his voice, it was a mere whisper. 'Oh God, you had this inside of you all along and still cared for me with such warmth . . .'

He fell silent and Ramya couldn't hold back her tears. She had hoped to feel light after the outburst, but Rohan's reaction had taken her by surprise. She had expected him to outright deny everything, and here he was, worried about how she must have felt through all of this!

After what seemed like eternity, when Rohan finally looked up, his face mirrored Ramya's agony. 'I wish I could go back in time and undo this, Ramya. I am so sorry, so ashamed of what I did. I don't want to blame it on booze or my age; nor do I want to dismiss it as locker-room talk. I take the blame. I was a self-absorbed jerk!'

Ramya was struck by Rohan's honesty, courage and the sheer grace to accept his folly without any ego or justification.

'After insulting your feelings with such cheap talk, I don't even know how to ask for forgiveness. I wish I could free you of the hurt you've carried all these years, Ramya.'

When their eyes met, Ramya saw her own pain roll down Rohan's cheek as a disobedient tear.

In that moment, she knew that she hadn't connected with anyone as deeply before.

~

Ramya woke up thinking about Rohan, just like old times. She had a compelling urge to protect him, help him create a new dream. Oh God, was she falling in love with him all over again?

Rohan woke up with mixed feelings. His heart was heavy with remorse for hurting Ramya, yet he was ready to fly. Ramya's tenderness, her smile, her touch, her warmth— everything about her made him feel alive! He wanted to take life head-on and figure out a new path.

Oh God, was he falling in love? Was he chasing another dream that may not come true?

She was twenty-eight; and he was thirty. They had both been touched by something pure and beautiful. And yet they were terrified of acknowledging it.

22

Our Story

Garima Bohra

As we were about to enter the enormous silver-polished gates of the classic Kubergarh Resort, my husband pulled me aside and tried to explain for the hundredth time . . .

'Look, it was a mistake, okay? And mistakes do happen. I mean, the names were the same, and that's why I got confused, which ultimately led to the exchange of orders.'

'Enough, Omi! You say one more word about that incident and I will walk out of this goddamned party!' I threatened him.

'Okay, fine. But can you smile? For me, please . . .' Omi said sheepishly.

His earnest request could not move me. I shrugged and walked in, holding my clutch tight to divert my anger.

The venue was magnificently spruced up with delicate white lilies and stunning pink gerberas. Lights shimmering from the giant chandeliers made the floor glitter like gold.

For a second I stared around in awe, feeling fascinated. It was a bash to celebrate the success of one of the beauty products Omi's company had launched a month back. Apart from the regular employees, the hall was full of well-known socialites and top models. Many people had gathered in thick packs around the rich and famous, trying hard to make connections.

We headed to the corner where Omi's friends were waiting for us with glasses of wine already clutched in their hands. The regular chit-chat and random jokes were circling around the table but a strange uneasiness enveloped me . . . The ear-bursting loud music began to cause the veins in my head to pound.

'Do you want something?' Omi sounded concerned as I stood up.

'Just need some fresh air. I will be back soon.'

'Wait, I will come with you.'

'No, you stay with your friends. I won't take long,' I said, dismissively.

'Please don't be mad at me for all that happened today,' Omi whispered in my ear.

I could not help rolling my eyes as I pushed him back into his chair and walked out into the garden.

The cool breeze was soothing. There was a juice bar under a freshly flowered nagchampa tree and I ordered some fresh orange juice for myself and gulped down half of it thinking about the eventful morning.

I had been fervently preparing and packing large orders of sweets, cookies and cupcakes with my staff for the past twenty-four hours for two of my important clients, who had been regulars since the early days of my catering business. And once, just once, I had asked Omi to deliver the packages. And what did he do? He switched them! This had never happened before. Both the customers, who used to write exceptionally good reviews on my website, dropped pretty harsh comments this time, pointing out how my business was becoming 'INEFFICIENT' and me 'CARELESS' with time.

And these blots were pretty difficult to erase from a customer's memory.

In the seven years of our marriage, Omi had tested my patience, sometimes more than our two beautiful children. His casual approach towards all things in life had always driven me crazy. He ate without caring about the extra layer of fat depositing around his waistline, wore the most mismatched clothes, scattered his files and papers everywhere in the bedroom, watched television shows at three in the morning, slept all afternoon on Sundays, pampered the children with ice cream and chocolate, forgot to ask for bills at stores, paid the maid in advance . . . the list was endless. But today, because of him, my reputation had received a blow. A bout of anger overwhelmed me and as I saw him through the glass wall, I felt like snatching the plate of snacks from him and dumping all of it on his head and punching him on his fat belly!

'Why do you look so angry?'

I turned around with a start and found Saahil Mehra staring at me. The same handsome features, the same robust physique and the same curly dark hair. He hadn't changed a bit! Saahil 'Charming' Mehra was a name discussed with great enthusiasm in the girls' dormitories even after we had started dating in the third year of our college. And although I didn't want to admit it, his killer looks had just made my heart skip a beat, again.

'Hi,' I managed to say and tucked a tuft of hair behind my ear.

'Good to see you after such a long time.'

'Likewise.'

'So do you work here?' he enquired.

'My husband does.'

'Oh . . . where is he?'

I looked through the glass wall at Omi and turned back to look at Saahil.

'He is around somewhere.'

I was a little embarrassed to introduce Omi to him. Saahil, after all, had been the rockstar of our college, the stylish hunk, whereas Omi was too plain, too simple. I was afraid that Saahil would mock me or judge me for marrying someone who was so average in appearance. They were complete opposites of each other. Saahil was fastidious about his lifestyle, his choices and his plans, whereas Omi had always been more of a carefree and spontaneous guy.

'What brings you here?' I enquired.

'I am one of the investors in this company.'

'That's nice.'

'Have you forgotten that grey makes you look fat?' Saahil stared at my evening gown and smiled sarcastically.

And the black tuxedo makes you look hot!

'No, it doesn't. And why would you still be interested in deciding which colour suits me?'

'Come on . . . After all, we were close a few years back.'

'Yeah, those were difficult times . . .'

'Really?' Saahil winked, making me blush.

'Yes,' I said, looking away.

'If you say so . . . but I am glad that my wife wears whatever I ask her to. Isn't she gorgeous?' Saahil pointed towards a stunning woman in a fiery-red gown, standing at a distance talking to a group of people.

'Hmm . . . so she likes being controlled,' I taunted.

'Some people, unlike you, are happy to do what they are told, Go-Go . . .'

'Don't call me that.'

'But you used to like it back then,' Saahil said, running his fingers through his hair.

'Now I don't.'

'Okay, I think I should leave now. My wife must be missing me. It was nice to see you after all this while, and I hope you are living on your own terms and making your own choices . . .'

'Yes.'

'Good for you. And good luck with your happy-happy life, Go-Go. Bye.' Saahil waved and walked away.

Happy-happy life? Really? Was I living one?

I waved back and finished my juice, watching him keenly as he approached his wife. A tuft of light brown hair fell on her beautiful face. Saahil stroked her cheeks lovingly as their eyes locked. A strong wave of jealousy surged inside me as they held hands, and then a deep regret filled my heart . . .

Saahil had been the most sought-after guy in our college and girls had been crazy about him. He was like a prince of dreams for most of them . . . For me too. His good looks and charm were bewitching. I had started liking him from the very first day of our college—the day he had walked into class for the first time and taken a seat near me. He had smiled as he had introduced himself—a smile I would have died for! With time we became good friends, but he had already conquered my heart. I never told him how I felt because I was too shy to confess my feelings and afraid of rejection. Meanwhile, he was busy getting in and out of relationships. And then, one fine day, while we were enacting a play at our college festival, he realized he had feelings for me. It was the happiest day of my life when he confessed his love for me.

Our relationship was precious to me and we were having a great time together, but things changed in a few months. Saahil the friend was very different from Saahil the lover. He was bossy and dominating, always wanting to do things his way—my opinions and desires never mattered to him. From deciding what I should wear to when I should call my parents, he had started controlling my whole life. It felt like living with a dictator. He always talked about his career and ambitions but would laugh off mine when I tried to discuss my dream of starting my own catering business someday. It was as if nothing related to my life mattered to him; it was suffocating and intolerable. And when I could not take it any more, I broke up with him, hurting his ego badly. Our relationship ended. Our paths changed. And he never called. And I was glad about it.

But today, after seeing him, old feelings stirred inside me. I started doubting my decision to leave him. Had I done the right thing? What harm would it have caused if I had just listened to him and given in to his dominating nature? So what if he wanted things his way? So what if he decided things for me? Would it have been that bad? Wouldn't my life have been better with him, instead of with this foolish Omi?

Saahil and I, we could have been the power couple of this evening. I would have been standing near him, holding his hand, certainly living a much more comfortable life, wearing fiery-red gowns and going to top-class parties. Things could have been different and wonderful . . .

'Hey, Gauri!' Richa hugged me from behind and said enthusiastically.

'What took you so long?' I asked.

She was Omi's junior and my good friend.

'Traffic. But I see you talked to Saahil Mehra. How do you two know each other?'

'We were at college together. You know him too?' I asked, a little surprised.

'Of course, honey. He is one of our major investors and, believe me, since he started pouring in his money, our profits have doubled. This guy is a magician!'

It was a little too much for me to take in in one night. Once again, I experienced a bout of envy for Saahil's wife. That woman had everything—not just the most handsome man of the party as her husband but also a share in the company!

'He is so good-looking . . . I wish he had married me!' Richa said dreamily.

I wish too . . .

'By the way, did you forgive Omi for the goof-up of orders?'

'Oh, please! He is the one at fault. He is the one who caused the ruckus and now he's asking his colleagues to defend him. I am fed up of Omi!'

'Come on, Gauri . . . It was because of the confusion in names . . .'

'He just gives excuses and does nothing.'

'Well, he did something phenomenal, actually . . . Although he asked me not to tell you, but I will.'

'What did he do now?'

'He did not come to office today and went to meet both your clients with flowers, and apologized to them. Also, he convinced them to delete their comments from your website and requested them to write good and honest reviews about the taste of your food.'

'Really?' I was taken aback.

'Check your website if you don't believe me. And if that was not enough, he asked all of us at the office to share your business page on our social media handles. The likes and hits on your site have spiked enormously!' Richa explained.

'That's amazing!' I smiled.

'That's love!' Richa winked.

I walked to Omi with a strange sense of joy. Suddenly, Saahil and his wife didn't matter . . . The life that I had imagined with him didn't matter. All the jealousy had disappeared—so had the regret. The hunger of wanting to be called a 'power couple' no longer prevailed. Omi was my present. He not only knew my dreams but cherished and respected them; he knew what made me happy. I sat near him and his face lit up as he saw me smile.

'What's that?' I asked, noticing a tag on the pocket of his shirt.

'We were playing a game and the anchor asked us to choose a tag for our respective spouses. You had gone out so I pinned it on my pocket,' he said, beaming from ear to ear.

My wife is my queen.

I tried to blink back the tears in my eyes. His smile, his innocence, his sincerity and even the tag said it all. He had always treated me like a precious gift. I mattered to him more than anything else. Yes, he acted weird; but sometimes even I did! He was not perfect, but neither was I. Our story had been a roller-coaster ride of joy and tears, love and fights, arguments and reconciliations—but as long as we were together, things would always be okay.

23

My Superhero Girlfriend

Writuraj Ghosh

People say that matches are made in heaven. And, in some cases, they are made somewhere close to heaven, around 32,000 feet above sea level. Imagine you are on a flight with the most beautiful girl you have ever met. You get to save that damsel in distress and become her hero. What if I tell you that it has happened with me? Sounds too good to be true, right? Well, this isn't any superhero story, and neither am I your friendly-neighbourhood Spiderman. But this story is worth telling.

Last Sunday I was returning from my hometown after attending my cousin's wedding. I had had so much fun in the past few days. Attending the wedding, catching up with school friends, enjoying the local street food and so much more! Thinking about the horrible traffic of Bengaluru, my blood-sucking boss and frequent power cuts waiting for me really made me upset. The only positive thing about returning to the city was that I was going to see Meera after two weeks. Meera and I have been dating for more than two years. After completing the security check, I grabbed a coffee for myself and took a seat in the waiting area.

I took out my phone and texted Meera. *I am at the airport. See you in three hours.*

Meera almost immediately replied: *Waiting for you, baby*. Which was followed by a couple of love emojis.

This lady always lifts up my mood. After texting for a while, I heard the boarding call. I boarded the flight and took my designated seat.

I am going on flight mode now. See you.

Have a safe journey. Don't forget to call me as soon as you land.

I checked her message and put my phone on flight mode. Then I closed my eyes and tried to get some sleep. The dreadful thought that I'd have to deal with my boss and the work pressure from the next day made its way back to my mind. And to add some special effects to my thoughts, a baby started crying from the seat behind me. I wished I could've stayed back a few more days.

'Excuse me.' I heard a female voice. I opened my eyes. A very beautiful girl was standing next to my seat. And when I say 'very beautiful', I mean real, natural and pure beauty. She looked like an Instagram model. Just that, in this case, it was a real person rather than a photo that was taken with a 100-megapixel camera and then further beautified by applying filters.

'Sorry to bother you, but may I take my seat, please?' She was pointing to the seat beside mine.

'Of course.' I stood up. I was on the aisle seat. She had the middle one. She stepped across me and took her seat. Immediately I realized that she smelt beautiful too. The fragrance of her perfume refreshed my mind. I could feel a weird pain in my chest. The pain was weird because I liked it. And my heart was beating faster. I could feel it. I took my seat and, in the process, our shoulders touched. Both the pain and the heartbeat doubled. I thought of talking to her, maybe offer help with the seat belt. But on second thoughts, I realized it was best to stay quiet. She was way out of my league. I looked around. An old lady was sitting at the window seat beside her. She was busy looking out of the window. The plane started moving. We were ready for take-off.

'Hi!' She was looking at me with a smile. Now my heart was racing faster than the plane. 'Sorry to bother you, but I am really scared of flying. Can we just talk for some time while the plane takes off?'

I didn't know what to say. I was dumbstruck for a couple of seconds. Then I started stammering, 'Ye . . . yes . . . yes . . . why not?'

'Are you a frequent flier?' she asked.

'Not frequent, but yes, once in three months on average. What about you?' Finally I was not stammering.

'Very rarely. I am not much of a traveller. Maybe once or twice a year.'

The plane was moving very fast on the runway. Things were shaking, my heart was pounding and then the most unexpected thing happened. As soon as the plane took off, she tightly grabbed my hand, which was on the armrest between the two seats. I could feel a current flow through my body. My heart was going to burst. I looked at her. Her eyes were closed. Her lips were moving, probably whispering some prayer, and her other hand was holding the other armrest. I kept looking at her. There were clouds outside and we started experiencing mild turbulence. Now I could feel her nails piercing my skin. Her back was straight, her legs were stiff and her beautiful face looked scared. The turbulence finally stopped. But she was still scared. I don't know what happened to me at that very moment. I put my other hand on top of hers, went really close to her and whispered into her ear, 'Hey, don't worry. Everything is going to be fine.'

I was really close to her. Her hair was falling on my face. She turned her face slowly towards me. Her eyes were still closed. Her lips were still moving. I could smell her strawberry lip gloss. Then she opened her eyes slowly. We kept looking at each other's eyes for a few seconds. I was getting lost in hers.

I suddenly came back to my senses and patted her hand. She realized that she was gripping my hand. She immediately removed her hand. 'I am so sorry. I don't know how this happened.'

'Relax! It's okay. How are you feeling now?' I asked while checking my hand. There were marks from her nails.

'Oh my God! I am so sorry!' Now she was looking apologetically at the marks.

'It's fine. Is this the first time you are flying alone?' I asked, smiling.

'Yes,' she replied. 'I shouldn't have. It was a stupid idea. I am afraid of heights and . . .' She was still looking at the nail marks on my hand.

'Hey! Look at me,' I interrupted. She looked up. 'Relax. Shit happens.'

She was smiling now. Finally! God, she was beautiful!

'Hope I haven't hurt you badly,' she asked.

'Hurt me? You almost killed me. When you held my hand, I almost had a heart attack.'

'Why?' she asked, laughing.

'You are so beautiful. Not even in my wildest dreams could I have imagined you holding my hand.' And we were both laughing.

We chatted throughout the flight. Her name was Anushka. She was returning from an official trip. She lived in Bengaluru and was working for a software company. She had a boyfriend but they had broken up two months back. She loved cats and was a huge fan of Virat Kohli. I told her a lot about me. Somehow I did not tell her about Meera. I was falling for her. I did not want to lose her. We were approaching Bengaluru. I didn't want the journey to end.

'Ladies and gentlemen, please fasten your seatbelts. We will be landing soon,' the pilot announced.

'If you are thinking of holding my hand again, please do it nicely. No more piercing,' I told her jokingly. To my surprise, she smiled back, held my hand and interlocked her fingers with mine.

'I am no longer scared. Thank you.'

Was she also falling for me? Some strange sense of confidence grew within me. I didn't feel like the guy any more who would shy away from talking to a beautiful girl. I felt worthy. I felt I was good-looking. I felt this was a new me. Till date, Meera was the most beautiful girl I had ever dated but, believe me, she was no match for Anushka when it came to looks. I realized that I was dating well below my standards. I kept looking at her with a smile on my face and a lot of thoughts inside my head.

The plane landed. We collected our luggage and came out of the airport, chatting all the while. We reached the Uber pickup point to board our cabs.

'Want to catch up again sometime?' I asked when she was about to board her cab. I was now confident that she liked me.

'I thought you were never going to ask,' she replied, smiling.

I took out my phone, unlocked it and smiled at her without saying anything. She took the phone and entered her number and asked me to call her.

She was about to turn around and board her cab when I called her again.

'Anushka!'

'Yes?' She turned around, smiling.

'I think I like you.' I didn't want her to leave.

'You think you like me?' she replied, stressing on the word 'think'.

'I mean, I really like you. I am sure of that.'

'I got to go now. My cab is waiting. By the way, I am free this Saturday,' she replied with a smile.

I felt tremendous joy inside me. We bid goodbye to each other and she boarded her cab.

I saved her number and was going to call her when Meera called.

'Hey! I told you to call me once you land. You forgot?' she asked.

I remembered she had told me so many times to call her as soon as I landed. I had totally forgotten. 'I am at the Uber pickup zone. I was going to call you after boarding the cab.'

'You idiot! I am at the airport. I came to pick you up. Thought it would be a surprise for you. And you were going to give me a shock.' She was laughing on the phone.

'Where are you?' I asked.

'Behind you, Mr Idiot.' I turned around and saw her walking towards me. My heart started pounding again. Had she seen Anushka? I was so screwed.

She ran the last few steps and hugged me tightly. 'Missed you so much.'

'I missed you too,' I replied.

'Come, let's go.' She grabbed my trolley bag and started walking.

I started walking with her. My head was messed up. I did not know what to say.

'We are going to my place now. There is another surprise waiting for you.' Meera was smiling. My head was still trying to process everything going on inside me.

'Don't tell me you have prepared my favourite mutton curry and jeera rice,' I asked.

'That was an easy guess.' She laughed. 'By the way, why didn't you call me when you landed?'

'I actually met an old friend of mine on the flight. I was talking to her and thought would call you once I board the cab.'

'That is one super-hot friend you got.' She winked at me with a smile.

'How did you know?' My heart stopped beating for a couple of seconds.

'I was waiting for you at the exit to surprise you. But then I saw the two of you coming out. You were laughing and talking to each other. So I decided to wait and surprise you after she leaves.' She unlocked the car and put the trolley on the back seat.

I was at a loss for words, my heart was pounding heavily and this was happening for the second time in three hours. 'You know what? Had it been someone else in your place, she would have been suspicious,' I said nervously while getting into the car.

'That is because that "someone else" does not know you as much as I do. I love you and completely trust you.' She smiled at me and turned on the ignition.

All this while when I was with Anushka, not for once did I think of Meera. There is no denying the fact that Anushka is really beautiful and we have many things in common. Whereas when it comes to Meera, we have very few things in common. Our taste in movies or music doesn't match. She likes beaches whereas I like mountains. Yet she cares for me, she trusts me blindly and loves me deeply.

Meera was driving and telling me about how she'd spent the last weekend with her friends, since I was not here. I was half listening and giving occasional nods and smiles. Maybe I was assuming things, and Anushka just wanted to be friends. Or maybe she wanted us to be more than that. But I didn't trust myself like Meera did. I was sure that I would fall for her with every passing day and would eventually ruin my relationship with Meera. The two hours that I spent in the flight with Anushka would be in my memories forever. But with Meera, I made memories every day. She was the one who forced me to go to the gym every day to stay fit. She was the one who took care of me when I met with an accident last year. She cared for me, she shouted at me and, most importantly, she inspired me to be a better person.

In the real world, superheroes don't wear capes or possess any superpowers. In the real world, superheroes are those people who become the pillars of your life without your knowledge. They make you a better person and are there for you even when you don't expect them to be. They don't give up on you even when you want to give up.

Sometimes imperfect relationships can make you happier than a perfect one can. I am thankful to Anushka, because I gained a confidence I thought I would never have. Maybe Anushka could have been my superwoman. But there was no confusion in my mind any more. I took out my phone and went to contacts. I searched for Anushka's name and deleted it without a second thought.

24

Arjun

Maria K Jimmy

Devotees flocked to the temple in the ungodly hours of the night. Lanterns were lit and a faint hint of jasmine and incense sticks lightened the tense atmosphere.

Kandanar Kelan, the fiery god, was running frantically around the court. Clad in a flowing straw skirt and awe-inspiring headgear, Kelan leapt into a bonfire and rolled in the flames. Frenzied drummers began beating in perfect synchronicity. Young priests lit palm-frond torches, swishing the embers into the air, and devotees recited hymns as Kelan screamed and performed his incredible *kalaasams** of the night. I held my breath. The flames were not singeing him, not even a little bit. The deity who had possessed him was Kandanar Kelan, a king of the yesteryears and a fearsome warrior god who had rendered him invulnerable and invincible.

---

* The dance steps in a performance.

He must have danced for minutes or hours—I still have no idea. Time seemed non-existent in the midst of such a captivating and soul-wrenching performance. The transformation from incorrigible wrath to raving ferocity, the dance was a sight to witness—a true explosion of music, dance and fervent devotion.

Towards the end, young boys fanned his sweaty body and priests brought him offerings of rice as the crowd broke up as fast as they had emerged, mumbling prayers and asking for blessings from the deity. The overall effect was distinctly supernatural and I figured that that was precisely the point.

Trying to figure out whether he was Kandanar Kelan at that moment or the fine young man of twenty-six that I knew was perplexing. Unsure, I walked towards him, scrutinizing his dazed expression and warm brown eyes.

'Arjun . . .' I called. It came out as a whisper, and even then I regretted saying it out loud. He looked at me, his tired, droopy eyes telling me that he had had enough for the night. I retreated.

Bali Theyyam is a popular dance form performed in small temples of northern Kerala, and Arjun was a Theyyam performer. Artistes like him are trained from an early age to carry out this divine profession. Years are spent learning the skills required for each part of the tradition. I knew him well, and I knew that he put his heart and soul into what he did. Arjun was tall, dark and handsome, with rough, masculine sandpaper hands. Outside of Theyyam, he was a different person altogether. His voice never lost its enthusiasm, his eyes were constantly observing in and out and his right cheek gave out dimples when he smiled.

It had been seven long months since I had met Arjun; it felt like forever, really, and one thing was certain—I was irrevocably and unconditionally in love with him.

I first ran into Arjun at a public library. I was surprised he liked to read. I was smitten by everything about him—his deep voice and warm brown skin, the way his nose twitched and the way he gestured with his palms as he talked. When he talked, his eyes bore right into you, as if deciphering every thought passing through your mind. It was mesmerizing, to say the least. He invited me to his temple shows and, soon, it turned out to be a routine affair for me. I grew to appreciate the brilliance of both the performance and the performer behind it.

The riverbank beyond the paddy field turned out to be our favourite place to loaf around. Early mornings were often swathed in silence, except for the mooing of the grazing cows with the egrets incessantly picking on their backs. Some days there would be sudden downpours and we would saunter in the softness of the monsoon rains as the wet mud gave away a fresh earthy scent.

We met behind moss-streaked walls and stole kisses in the corners of the overgrown gardens of the countryside. We watched sunsets together as he traced his fingers along the nook of my elbow. He would narrate mythical stories from the past as I leaned against his shoulder, letting the legend of the god of the Aasharis sink in.

Arjun was a wonder. He made me laugh and he made me think. He told me how this divine profession had been handed down to him through his family line and that even though he didn't exactly *choose* it, it was an integral part of him—something he could never let go of. He told me how turning into Kandanar Kelan was a state of trance, a state of frenzy, and that nothing gave him more ecstasy than being taken over by an ancient spirit that people worshipped to this day.

Some days Arjun liked to dive head first into his notions and I secretly loved the way his eyebrows knit together when he was in deep thought.

'Theyyam is a cultural war cry,' he would say, sipping on his hot *kattan kaapi** in the early hours of the morning, 'against firmly rooted notions of caste hierarchies.'

'Basically, Theyyam continues to raise pertinent questions between the equations of the higher and the lower castes in Kerala,' I would chime in, trying to sound intelligent and oh-so desperate to impress him. Arjun would nod.

'It is no more a dying art,' he would add slowly. 'It changes with time.'

Once, I noticed a dab of orange paint from the previous night's performance still smeared on his face. I reached down to wipe it and we both laughed light-heartedly.

I used to attend all of Arjun's performances at the *kshetram*†, and several days I even stayed back after the show, despite him pushing me away every time. He liked to be alone right after the show but I liked to push it. It just didn't feel right to leave him alone then.

---

* Black coffee.
† The temple where a performance takes place.

'Please go home, Lilly,' he would whimper softly in between breaths. 'This metamorphosis isn't going to get any easier if you stick around.'

It was painful to see the struggle, the staggering combat between his true self and the raging Kelan, who was killed hundreds of years ago.

That day was different, though. I had told him that we had to talk, that I had overstayed my visit, that it was almost time for me to head back home and that we needed to sort things out. I knew it was sudden, but at some point I had to tell him. We were two people from really different backgrounds and we both knew that right from the beginning.

Arjun was unusually quiet. He didn't ask me to not leave. He didn't offer to talk to my parents about us. He didn't even react to the quiet agitation in my voice. He did none of the things I had expected him to do. He lifted the corner of his crisp white *mundu**, crossed his leg and merely nodded at what I had said, as if I had lightly mentioned something that didn't concern him at all.

Something broke inside me. I bit my lip until I tasted blood. I felt a sense of betrayal. And, for the first time since I had been with Arjun, a pang of remorse pricked me inside.

Later that night, we met by the ebony river. Words did not escape either of us. The air was thick and the silence was unusually deafening.

We sat by the riverbank like we always did. The river pulsed behind us, glistening in the moonlit night. His arm

---

* A garment worn around the waist.

was cold, unfamiliar, and his eyes were down—unsmiling, lost and pondering. He was in pain—I could feel it.

The calm of the night reawakened our senses to new melodies and we wrapped our arms against each other delicately, as though sheltering each other from the pain that was seeping in. Two brown bodies—a man and a woman enchanted by love yet divided by the brutal differences that societal normalcy teaches us.

Yet what do they know about love? They teach us that love is financial stability, that love is the union of two families, that love is a flimsy match between two matrimonial profiles.

They don't know that real love is blind, that it sees no caste, no gender, no race, no colour, no age, no materialism.

And yet how far was it worth to get hurt, to get jeered at, to get lectured—for love?

Was love worth all the pain, all the torment, all the misery?

Something inside me whispered 'yes' and yet I didn't trust myself with it.

'Lilly,' Arjun whispered, his soft marble lips on my ear, breaking me free from my tangential thoughts. Perhaps he knew what I was thinking. Perhaps he, too, was thinking the same things. Perhaps he could read my mind. I liked to believe that we had that charismatic connection between us. I liked to think that it was what had brought us together in the first place.

'Lilly . . . Lilly . . . Lilly . . .' he kept mumbling my name like it was the last time he would ever say it. Like he was discovering unique ways to utter my little two-syllable name. Every time he drawled my name with his tongue, I felt warm inside. I felt like my name made more sense. It felt precious; *I* felt precious. It felt so surreal, like we were both in a dream—two goldfishes, swimming surreptitiously in calm blue waters, swishing our long, flowy mermaid tails, serene and carefree and blissful.

'Hey,' he said softly, snapping me out of my thoughts again. His softness made me wonder if his exceptional avatar was all a big lie. How could a human being so gentle transform himself into a screeching god plunging into flames at the drop of dusk? It was all a big mystery to me—a mystery that was better knotted up and dropped into the bed of the ocean and never thought of again. After all, all questions don't have answers.

Crickets chirped and moths flew, and I gave in to the unending gush of my contemplations. Bamboo sticks swayed in the summer breeze and I snuggled in his arms till sleep carried us both to nirvana.

The next evening, Arjun was at the temple singing and chanting mantras, and I immediately knew that I had lost him. His eyes were shut in deep prayer and I couldn't help wondering if he was doing that on purpose, trying to shield himself from anything that stopped him from his animistic fire dance. Would he shut his eyes to me too? The thought terrified me.

At night he once again got into the skin of Kandanar Kelan. It was the only thing he knew—the only thing that made him *him*. He painted his face in intricate designs of red and orange, and wore the elaborate costume he had made out of silk and coconut husks. His antique silver necklace shone in the darkness. He tightened his metal anklets that clinked as he strutted to the courtyard of the kshetram, mystifying the ambience further. He swayed to the cataclysmic drumbeats of the chenda* and lost himself to the legend of Kandanar Kelan, a universal energy vibrating from inside of him. Onlookers hummed in both prayer and awe.

It was just another night of Kelan leaping over fires and instilling fear into the hearts of his people. Of Kelan showing his rage to the fire that burnt him to death years ago.

Yet that night was different for me. For us. When the spirit of Kelan took over his body that night and Arjun entered his phase of trance, it was I who jumped into the burning pyre.

It was my body that burnt instead of his.

My insides scorched.

My head throbbed.

My tongue was parched.

My skin was singed by the flames.

It could be the very last I saw of Arjun.

Or maybe life would surprise us in the most mysterious ways.

Nevertheless, Kandanar Kelan screeched and danced his heart out that night. The forest fire that killed Kelan hundreds of years ago must have been ashamed of itself.

---

* A percussion-like instrument played in the southern parts of India.

25

Love in the Times of Marriage

Aparajita Shishoo

When Adil saw her across the room, his heart skipped a beat. He couldn't take his eyes off Meera's radiant face. He decided to walk up to her.

'Hi,' Adil said.

Meera was standing alone, enjoying the party her friend, Kanika, had thrown. Meera turned to look at Adil and smiled back at him with a soft 'hi'.

Adil continued, 'You seem to be the arty-farty type. What are you doing at a filmy party?'

Meera was a bit tipsy by that time, so she retorted, 'I am definitely farty, but with some arty. What about you?'

Adil laughed out loud at her candour and asked her again what she was doing at such a party.

'I am fishing for some juicy stories for my publication. You?'

'I am trying to *make* some juicy stories!' Adil winked at Meera.

Meera laughed and asked, 'Are you flirting with me?'

'Are you noticing?' Adil said.

Meera shot back, 'I am ignoring . . . I don't flirt with boys who have just entered puberty.'

'Oh! That hurt . . . really hurt!' Adil said, imitating a heartbreak. 'By the way, I am twenty-five, well beyond my puberty years.'

Meera laughed again at Adil's dramatics, and they continued their conversation.

Adil was a cinematographer in the Hindi film industry and the camera was his first love, but right now his own lenses were fixed on Meera's face. 'So what brings you to Mumbai?'

'Change,' said Meera, after a pause.

'Change from what—scenery, job, ex-boyfriend? Ahem, ahem . . .'

Meera smiled. 'Are you trying to find out whether I have a boyfriend?'

Adil flushed a little. 'No, I am just . . . you know . . . trying to keep the conversation going . . .'

Meera just laughed at his bumbling behaviour and walked towards the balcony. Adil followed her.

At the other end of the room, Kanika noticed the chemistry between the two and was happy that her friend was finally enjoying flirting and chatting up guys. Meera had been fed up of constantly being badgered to get married, and had decided to shift to Mumbai and take a break from meeting boys—one worse than the other.

Conformity and Meera had never gone hand in hand. She had always gone against the tide, and so, when she chose the media and not the medical profession, it did not come as a surprise to her parents—father a banker and mother a college professor. They were always supportive of her choices and let the freedom-loving girl be.

'So, I see Adil has taken a liking to you,' Kanika said, giving Meera a cup of tea the next morning.

Meera looked at her as she took the cup and ignored the suggestion with a wave of her hand.

'What?' said Kanika. 'I am telling you, he is smitten. He couldn't take his eyes off you. He has fallen for you— and I could also see a spark in your eyes.'

Meera listened to her friend patiently and said, 'First, I am thirty-two years old, and I have no interest in "boys" and second . . . I don't know . . . he is from a different religion—not that it matters to me, but still . . . You know how society is . . .'

'Madam, this is Mumbai—young, old doesn't matter in this city. Actually it shouldn't—and doesn't—matter anywhere, except in your head. And second, religion and society—when have these things mattered to you?'

Meera's thoughts went to her time in Delhi, when she was cruising along at twenty-six and had suddenly been sucked into the vortex of marriage. As was the tradition in India, when you turned a certain age, you were supposed to find a stranger, tick the necessary boxes in the list and get married. It was always about the right age, and adjustments to turn the stranger into the right partner along the way.

Meera was always clear that it would be companionship that would make her settle down and not societal stamp, but despite this conviction, her life had started revolving around that one word—marriage. From family gatherings to the Holi-Diwali gatherings, every place became a meeting ground for boy talk. But Meera did not budge; nor did her parents, who supported her decision.

Meera's reverie was broken when her phone pinged. Kanika gave her a mischievous look, pointing at the message that had just come from Adil: *Good morning, Ms Newspaper!* Meera smiled.

Kanika started singing a song from a popular Hindi film and Meera hit her with a pillow. Laughing, Kanika picked up the tea mugs and left the room.

With Kanika gone, Meera turned her attention to the text and replied: *I work in a magazine, not a newspaper.*

Ah! One and the same thing.

Okay, if it is the same thing, I will call you Mr Photographer.

Chalega, *as long as you call me.*

Meera laughed and blushed at the same time, and sent him a laugh emoji. She then got up to get dressed for office.

While in the cab, Meera's mind went back to some of the people she had met. Vikram Singh. Meera had met him only because he was the son of somebody her father knew. He was an interior designer and looked like a good prospect. But to the utter dismay of her family, Vikram had turned out to be quite a dud. He had told Meera, '*Yaar, tu to journalist hai* . . . I want a 70 per cent homely girl. *Tu to kab ayegi, kab jayegi . . . aisa to nahi chalega, na, shaadi ke baad* (You are a journalist and I want a 70 per cent homely girl . . . There will be no time to when you come or go . . . this won't work after marriage).'

Then there was Akash, who had made tall claims of being intrigued by her work and trying to know her, but Meera later realized that his father, who would regularly check their mails, did not approve of her.

Then there was Prateek, the investment banker who just couldn't stop drinking, and, ultimately, Meera had realized he was just trying to get over his ex.

Once she had met a lawyer—she couldn't even remember his name—who had thought that Meera's driving with her girlfriends across northern India was very adventurous and that his 'Mummy-ji' would never allow it.

As soon as she got out of her cab, her phone beeped again.

Hello, Ms Newspaper, can we meet for coffee today?

Meera smiled. *Why?*

What do you mean why? I want to meet you, that's why.

Yeah, so I am asking, why do you want to meet me?

There was no reply from the other side, so Meera let it be. She got busy in her work, but constantly kept checking her phone. Finally, around 5 p.m., her phone rang. It was Adil.

'So, Ms Newspaper . . . Why I want to have coffee with you is because I have never met a more engaging person than you in my life.'

Meera smiled to herself and said, 'Sorry, can't hear you. Can you be a little louder?'

Adil repeated, 'Because I have never met a more engaging person.'

' . . . Sorry, can't hear you . . .'

Adil repeated, ' . . . Most engaging person . . .'

Meera started laughing and Adil finally understood that she was teasing him and he laughed with her.

In the next hour, Meera reached the designated coffee shop.

There was an awkward moment when they both didn't know whether to hug or to shake hands. Finally they decide on a half-hug and sat down. They ordered coffee and Adil began by telling Meera a little more about himself.

'So you get excited about international projects . . . Beautiful women and amazing locations. What more does one want?' Meera teased him.

'I am not into beautiful bodies; I like brains. I like conversations about films, about life, sometimes random talks, sharing childhood memories and sometimes toilet humour . . . These are the areas I specialize in,' Adil replied naughtily.

'Ugh! Gross! Who does that?' Meera made a face.

Adil replied with a hint of pride, '*Arre,* I do . . . It's very enjoyable. *Aap dheere dheere mujhse milti rahengi to aap bhi enjoy karne lagengi* (Once you start meeting me more often, even you'll start enjoying it).'

'So that means I'll have to meet you again?' Meera said, as if horrified by the idea.

To which Adil made a sad puppy face while nodding his head in the affirmative.

After this meeting, chats and phone calls became frequent between them. Although Meera was initially reluctant to let things grow between them, Adil always drew her into conversation and made her feel relaxed. It had been a few months but, to Meera's surprise, neither had Adil made a move on her, nor had he gotten bored of her. She'd always thought either of this would happen naturally, considering the age difference between them. And that would be the time their relationship would end. Meera was always confused about his behaviour, but she also liked the fact that he never crossed a line and was always playfully flirting with her. Theirs was a lovely bond that had raw attraction mixed with fun, which made both of them very comfortable in each other's company.

Meera was now also used to his toilet humour, which was disgusting but also made her laugh. He was one of a kind and she realized she really did enjoy his company. But, then again, her mind had its own doubts and questions.

One day when she and Kanika were out shopping, Adil came up in conversation. Kanika started teasing Meera about him. 'He is nice, but he is a kid . . .' said Meera.

'Well, he can produce kids if you want,' replied Kanika. Meera hit her friend playfully at the suggestion but at the same time blushed.

'No, c'mon . . . Give me one good reason why you aren't jumping into bed with him. And I can guarantee you he is a good guy . . . No hanky-panky. You are a thirty-two-year-old woman; he is a twenty-five-year-old boy. No reason you guys shouldn't be together. Please don't give me that age and religion and family and society and film-industry crap!' reprimanded Kanika.

As Meera started to say something, Kanika added, 'Take a leap of faith, Meera.'

'But, Kanika, I have known him just a few months.'

'So?' her friend retorted. 'Haven't you heard of love at first sight? And who's asking you to get married? You have always stuck to your guns and not succumbed to the pressures of being with just about anyone. And now if you have someone who wants to take a chance on you, then why are you being a *bargad ka ped* (a banyan tree)?'

Meera silently heard out her friend.

Kanika continued, 'And I don't think it is just an initial spark for him, because it's been about five months and he hasn't made any untoward move. All he wants is to spend some quality time with you and enjoy your company . . . I don't think it is too much to ask for. And if this goes somewhere, why the hell not?'

Suddenly Meera's phone beeped. *Hello, Ms Newspaper, can we meet for coffee today?*

Meera couldn't help but smile. There was something very reassuring in Adil's simple message today. Suddenly all her apprehensions vanished, the spark was reignited, the blood went rushing to her cheeks, her heartbeat quickened and thoughts of society went into the trash can.

Of course, she texted back.

26

Love Is Coming Soon . . .

Kiran Wingkar

Four months after their wedding . . .

When Deepti woke up, Ravi was still asleep beside her. He was in a deep slumber and looked like a child sleeping. She wanted to give him a morning kiss but wasn't sure how he would react. Would he like it or get upset? They were yet to understand each other. She thought it would be better not to. Then she headed to the kid's bedroom, where her three-and-a-half-year-old prince, Shourya, was sleeping. She gave him a peck on the cheek. He was also in deep sleep.

As she sat alone in the balcony, enjoying the view of the garden and sipping on hot chocolate milk, Deepti worried about the nausea she had been experiencing over the past week. Her mother, who had spoken to her last evening, suggested doing a pregnancy test because Deepti had missed her date as well. She recalled the words of her 3 a.m. friend:

'You both are having a hard time with each other. Do not even think about a child right now.'

Three months before their wedding . . .

It was 2 p.m. and Deepti was driving. She felt miserable. After all, she was going to attend a silly event that she had never imagined she would attend in her lifetime. It was a remarriage meet-up arranged by a matrimonial company. Her father had emotionally blackmailed her into going with the only weapon he had—her son from her previous marriage.

'You have to do it for your son. He will get a father. Haven't you seen his expressions when he sees his friends' fathers?' he had said.

She was still not convinced, though. It had been two years that her husband had died. She had moved on, but could not imagine anybody else in his place. However, she was also missing a companion in her life. Whenever she would ask her girlfriends to go for an outing, they would make up excuses saying they already had plans with their husbands. She still kept her husband's favourite perfume in her closet. The scent gave her a sense of his presence. She felt lonely, though she was surrounded by the people she loved.

Deepti reached the venue on time but was nervous.

How will I face other men who are willing to marry me?

She was given a number badge and a table number at the registration counter. She wore her badge and went to the assigned table. A man was already seated there, wearing her lucky number 9. She was not ready to talk. He was tall, dark and handsome—but she thought he was too tall for her 5-foot-1 frame and that he would look like 6 feet beside her.

As the evening wore on, she met other men as well, most of whom were divorced. As she talked to each of them, she realized why their wives must have left them. That tall, dark and handsome guy's story, however, was intriguing. He was also divorced, though his first was a love marriage. He sounded reasonable to her, and she was curious to know why he was single. Other than him, she did not find any of the other men attractive.

A couple of days later, she found a marriage proposal from the tall, dark and handsome man in her mailbox. She studied his profile. He was a deserving candidate—he had a job with a handsome salary, had his own house and was a fitness freak to boot! He had already registered himself for the 'Ironman' race. She remembered her high-school crush, Milind Soman, who was the only Ironman she had known so far.

His name was Ravi Kulkarni. They decided to talk on the phone. When Deepti called Ravi, he was going to Ooty for an ultramarathon, which she found quite impressive. Her first question was whether he would be ready to accept her son. He said yes. That was the only condition she had. She was hesitant to ask about his divorce. He sensed this and clarified that his ex-father-in-law was against their marriage from the start and had somehow convinced his daughter to divorce him a couple of years after their marriage. Ravi spoke reasonably on the phone as well. They decided to meet a month later.

Two months before their wedding . . .

She went alone to meet him. They had decided to have lunch together. During lunch, they shared the expectations they had from each other. His expectation was to have his own child from her. Deepti agreed, thinking it was a fair expectation.

She asked him, 'What will you do if your ex wants to come back into your life?'

A smile appeared on his face. He said to her, 'I was in love with her. But the way she behaved with me and my parents, I would never accept her again.'

They got along well and decided to marry in court.

Deepti was on cloud nine, reliving the bygone era of talking for hours on the phone. She was so happy. They talked for hours at night. They talked about their past, their likes, their dislikes, and so on.

One month before their wedding . . .

One day, Ravi came to meet Deepti. They were talking and laughing, but Ravi seemed restless. Deepti had parked her car on an empty road. She wanted some quiet time with him. Every place they went to was crowded. She was saying something when, all of sudden, he grabbed her hands, pulled her into his arms and pressed his lips against hers. She got butterflies in her stomach. Immediately, she pulled herself back from his arms into the driving seat. She had not expected this. They remained quiet for some time. She was not angry. In fact, she had quite enjoyed the romantic moment.

Twenty days before their wedding . . .

As the days passed, the length of their talks got shorter and shorter. She found it strange. In her previous marriage, the talks had increased with each passing day. As time passed, Ravi became merely a passive listener during their phone calls. He would ask Deepti to talk, but she could not find any subject to talk about on some days. She sensed something was not right.

A day before their wedding . . .

Deepti was waiting for her mehendi artist when she got a message from Ravi's cousin. His cousin wanted to tell her something. Puzzled, Deepti started reading.

His ex-wife was a good person. She was close to me. They got separated because they wanted different things in life. He suffered a lot due to his blunt and straightforward nature. You have to teach him how to behave with kids. He doesn't have experience with kids. I suggest you find some common interest so that you can spend quality time with each other. Initially, keep your finances separate.

Deepti kept reading the text messages. She was perplexed.

Is he the right person or have I taken this decision in a hurry? she thought. *How bad could he be?*

The mehendi artist entered. Her chain of thought broke.

On their honeymoon . . .

Deepti and Ravi had decided to go to Shimla and Kullu–Manali for their honeymoon. Their honeymoon was unlike any other couples' honeymoon. It was more like a family trip, because they were yet to understand each other. The situation got even more challenging when Deepti decided to take her son, Shourya, along. Throughout the trip, she was occupied with her son. Ravi was annoyed by Shourya's mischiefs and irritated since he did not get enough time with Deepti alone. But he masked his feelings and focused, instead, on trying to build memories with her.

Ravi knew that Deepti used to be a sportsperson. He managed to persuade her to try out the adventure sports in Manali. To their surprise, she completed them all with ease, compared with other participants, including Ravi. It was then that she remembered the outspoken, mischievous and adventurous Deepti, who had been lost somewhere all those years due to family commitments. She told Ravi how happy she was that day and expressed her gratitude to him for encouraging her to try the sports.

On their way back to the hotel, Ravi said to her, 'You'll find it strange, but I'm not like other husbands who put loads of expectations on their wives—whether it be preparing a nice hot breakfast every morning or satisfying me in bed. I will never put any restriction or compulsion on you for family commitments. However, I've developed a set of goals based on my hobbies that I passionately want to fulfil in due course of time. I also encourage you to develop some hobbies that make you happy as well. We are two different people; it is important for us to have separate interests. I don't want you to ignore your interests for me.'

One month after their wedding . . .

He stopped calling her in the afternoons from office. Romantic messages were out of the question. His Ironman race was around the corner and training was on in full swing. Due to this, he would often come home late. Even his weekends were reserved for training. Deepti was disappointed their honeymoon phase had ended so soon. Her husband had no time for her, even though his reason was genuine. The Ironman race was one of the reasons she had accepted his proposal. Though her husband had no time for her, she was free to do anything she wanted. She started socializing with the people of her society and exploring the new city, where she had shifted after her second marriage. Ravi and Deepti were both immersed in their own worlds. But they had amazing nights together. Their chemistry in bed was undeniable. She realized that for passionate lovemaking, love was not necessary.

While Deepti enjoyed her life as an individual, she missed the kind of family life she had had in her first marriage. Her first husband and she had so many common interests that they did not have any individual interests. It was hard for her to come to terms with this new marriage. Yet, she worked hard to keep herself busy and portrayed herself as an independent woman in front of him. She didn't want to show him that she needed him in the marriage, more than anything else. Soon, ego clashes became the most common reason for their daily fights. During one such fight, he warned her: 'This marriage was just an adjustment for me. Do not try to pull me into it.'

And he left for his official tour.

Her heart sank. She cried her heart out and began to realize the relevance of the messages Ravi's cousin had sent her on the day of her mehendi. She did not want to talk to Ravi or see his face any more. Deepti remembered her 3 a.m. friend and called him for advice.

Deepti told her 3 a.m. friend the whole story of her second marriage and the difficulties she was facing. Her friend listened to everything and said:

Living an independent life is not a crime, as long as he isn't putting any restrictions on you. He is letting you live the way you want. Both of you are from different backgrounds. That girl left him, and everyone, including his own relatives, judged him during his bad time. If I were in his place, I would have been devastated. I think he is a very courageous man. I don't think he would trust any other woman so easily. I have met him at your wedding; he is a nice, reasonable guy. Give him some time. All your fights are ego clashes. Your ego is ruining your relationship. Keep your ego aside. Nowadays, women are self-sufficient. They are able to take care of themselves. Isn't it true? I mean, if he restricts you from doing something, will you listen to him? No. Why would you? You take responsibility for your own actions. Look at your mom and dad—your dad cares so much for your mom. He does this because he knows that she can't do anything without his help. Does this apply in your case? Let him care for you first. Love will follow. You are both having a hard time with each other. Do not even think about a child right now.

Deepti listened to him carefully and began to understand her husband's point of view. She pondered her friend's words the entire afternoon. 'Yes, I was economically dependent on my first husband for some years of our marriage. That's why things went smoothly,' she thought.

She wanted to do whatever it took to make this marriage work. At night, Ravi gave her a call. He spoke as if nothing had happened in the morning. She responded normally as well.

As the days passed, Deepti would deliberately make small mistakes in her tasks, due to which Ravi started to believe that Deepti might need his assistance in some of her important tasks. A sense of care started getting established between them. To take it to the next level, Deepti started to take his opinion in her important decisions. Talking to him about what had happened in her office was her routine. Ravi also started sharing with her events of his day at work and his fitness routine. Day by day the communication between them grew. They started liking each other's company like friends. They did not realize when they started to pour their hearts out to each other.

Four months after their wedding . . .

Sitting alone in the balcony and sipping the hot chocolate, Deepti realized that a small compromise on her ego changed the situation around her dramatically. She knew this was just the beginning and that there were miles to go before winning his love and trust. Old ladies say, 'A child can bring your partner closer.' So she thought, 'If I am pregnant, this will be another step towards Ravi's heart.'

She believed that love was coming soon . . . She was sure of it.

Contributors

Dayal Punjabi is a self-published writer and poet. His debut collection under his pen name Amaranthine Poetry, *Notes from the Heart*, became a bestseller on Kindle India. He currently serves as the content head at Storiyaan.com

Sucharita Date is an undergraduate student in Chennai. Her love for reading inspired her to take up writing at the age of sixteen. She has since written a number of short stories, mainly for children, as well as poetry, and has been working on a novel for the past few months. She aspires to publish a book one day. When she is not reading or writing, Sucharita likes to spend her time cycling, trekking and listening to Billy Joel.

Sai Nithin can usually be found reading a fantasy novel in the last bench of his class. He enjoys gazing at the stars and riding his bicycle with his earphones plugged in. One of his dreams is to see his name printed on the cover of a novel. He lives in Hyderabad and is pursuing his college degree. He can be contacted at sainithink08@gmail.com

Ruby Gupta is the bestselling author of eight books, including the murder mystery *No Illusions in Xanadu* published by Bloomsbury, the suspenseful *A Degree in Death* (long-listed for the Crossword Book Award) and the mystical *Maya: A Novel*. Her books on technical communication, published by Cambridge, are part of the syllabi of various universities. An awardee of the Group Study Exchange programme for the US by Rotary International, she is also the recipient of the Pratibha Samman Award. She is professor and HoD, Humanities, at the Indian Military Academy, Dehradun.

Anuj Dutt is a writer of short stories, articles and poems. He has been writing since he was twelve years old. He stays in Bengaluru with his two daughters, wife, a dachshund and a pug. He is passionate about animal welfare, amateur radio and *Sherlock Holmes*. He is currently 'curating' a detective in the pages of his notebook, which he believes could overshadow Karamchand and Sherlock Holmes one day.

Rachita Ramya is an author, a practising public health researcher, and a dentist by training. She has worked on projects on mental health and health disparities. Rachita's debut book, *Radical Politics of Indian Love*, has also won an award in a writers' group in California, the US. She lives with her sister in New York City, who is a scientist at the New York Stem Cell Foundation.

Rupali Tiwari graduated as a homoeopath in 2015, but couldn't digest the mundane lifestyle of having a full-time job or running her own clinic. Books have been her solace since childhood. She pursued her passion to write after she completed her studies. Over the years, her stories have been a source of entertainment, inspiration and awe among her friends and family, and she often comes out of her shell to share it with the world.

Pooja Dubey is an author, psychologist, strategist, researcher and trainer with more than thirteen years of experience in writing. She left no stone unturned to develop her skill in writing and has an indefatigable capacity to produce different forms of writing, which include fiction, non-fiction, poetry, and content in the academic, technical, creative, business, marketing, philosophical and spiritual domains.

Aarthika Mathialagan is a twenty-two-year-old literature student who loves to read and watch fiction. She loves to review novels and even won the first prize in a book-review competition.

Mohammad Afroz is an engineer by profession and a storyteller by heart. When his Hogwarts letter didn't arrive when he was eleven, Dumbledore himself introduced him to a different kind of magic— books. And one day he hopes to lend the same magic to people in need through the stories he writes.

Praneetha Gutta is a software engineer by profession and a writer by passion. If she is not in front of her laptop doing her office work, she is either sitting with a book or in front of the television. Her other works include *You Are Mine: So Are Your Dreams Too* and a short story named 'It's Time to Regret'. Currently, she is active on Wattpad and StoryMirror, where you can read her stories and poems. She also loves watching cricket, especially when M.S. Dhoni is at the crease. You can reach her at pranupinky7@gmail.com and on Instagram @book_lover789

Supreet Kaur is a corporate consultant during day and a writer at night. Charming yet emotionally complex, she channelizes her emotions through writing. She gets her writing skills from her dad, who is an avid poet. Supreet wrote her first poem under his guidance when she was six years old. She runs an Instagram writing page and blog with the name '_writerscorner'.

Suranya Sengupta is an opinionated feminist, an Instagram poet and an ardent blogger on 'A Journey to Discover Life'. She has a passion for history and stories, which she wants to share with the world from her corner in Kolkata. Words are her preferred weapon of choice to make a difference.

Sarbani Ray is a blog and webzine writer, who writes both in English and in her native language, Bengali. Her first published work is a Bengali fiction, *Kono Ek*. An engineer by profession, she has worked in the public sector with a leading power generator of India for more than twenty-five years. She also holds an MBA degree from Warwick Business School, the UK, and specializes in global energy management. An avid reader of all kinds of books, writing has been her passion for a long time. Sarbani loves music, travel, creating new ideas and exploring new horizons.

Sashwati Ghosh is an architect and planner based in Kolkata and Milan, and a strong believer in sustainable living. She loves all creative and passionate pursuits, including reading, writing, cooking, travel and dance. She is a compulsive dreamer and her companions of choice are good books, strong coffee and the rains!

Mariam Rashid is an aspiring poet and a writer from Aligarh. She is currently busy collecting verses and stories, and the colours she sees on the streets of Aligarh. She desires to pour beautiful stories and verses of love and peace into the vessel of this world.

Krusha Sahjwani Malkani is a Mumbai girl with a dream to #WriteTheWorldPink. She heads business in the APAC region for a leading employee-communication platform, Sociabble, and is the co-founder of an initiative called The Pink Thread, which celebrates and empowers women in corporate India. You can read her thoughts and catch updates on her books on her Instagram page @write_the_world_pink

Hamsini R. loves filter coffee, enjoys singing and spends far too much time watching Korean dramas, when not absorbed in the latest page-turner. A corporate stooge by day and scribbler by night, Hamsini specializes in awkward social interactions and is petrified of small talk. Hamsini lives in Bengaluru with her husband and dreams of living in the countryside with two cats, a dog and a goat.

Kaustubhi Singh relishes reading as a means to understanding the world. As she reads more, she realizes that the ability to change the world lies in the power of words. That was what made her venture into writing.

Nandita Warrier is a corporate consultant, a leadership coach and a wellness enthusiast. A 'butterfly in the making', she is finding her wings as an author and wants to entertain and inspire the world through her writing.

Garima Bohra is a homoeopathic physician with a passion for writing. Many of her short stories have been published in a leading English magazine. She also has a published novel to her credit. She lives in Jodhpur with her family.

Writuraj Ghosh is a true Bengali, which explains his love for food, art and football. He is a bit of an introvert, but once he is friends, it is difficult to make him stop talking. In his leisure time, which is very rare, he likes to read or watch movies.

Maria K. Jimmy was born and brought up in Kochi, Kerala. She is a medical student, an avid reader, a major overthinker and a bossy elder sister to her three siblings. She is a full-time daydreamer who romanticizes the bittersweet ache of existence.

Aprajita Shishoo has worked with brands such as *Hindustan Times* and *India Today*. She moved to Mumbai to pursue a career as a writer and a film-maker. She currently works as a producer for a media house in Mumbai. She loves to read biographies, thrillers, political non-fiction, light romance and classics. She spends her weekends either chilling with Netflix or with friends.

Kiran Wingkar is an instructional designer from Bengaluru. Creating engaging content for viewers is part of her job. She gets excited about sharing her life experiences with the world.